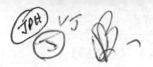

THE SECRET OF SHEARWATER

When Zoe Carson inherits a cottage in Cornwall, she takes a holiday from her job in London to stay at the cottage. There, she makes friends with the local people, including the hot-tempered Gregory Enodoc. Zoe is glad of their friendship when events take a sinister turn and the police become involved. And when she decides to leave London to live permanently at the cottage, Zoe is unaware of the dangers into which this will lead her . . .

Books by Diney Delancey
in the Linford Romance Library:

FOR LOVE OF OLIVER
AN OLD-FASHIONED LOVE
LOVE'S DAWNING
SILVERSTRAND
BRAVE HEART
THE SLOPES OF LOVE

DINEY DELANCEY

THE SECRET OF SHEARWATER

Complete and Unabridged

LINFORD
Leicester

First published in Great Britain in 1982 by
Robert Hale Limited
London

First Linford Edition
published 2007
by arrangement with
Robert Hale Limited
London

British Library CIP Data

Delancey, Diney
  The secret of Shearwater.—Large print ed.—
Linford romance library
  1. Cornwall (England: County)—Fiction
  2. Romantic suspense novels
  3. Large type books
  I. Title
  823.9'14 [F]

  ISBN 978–1–84617–717–0

Published by
F. A. Thorpe (Publishing)
Anstey, Leicestershire

Set by Words & Graphics Ltd.
Anstey, Leicestershire
Printed and bound in Great Britain by
T. J. International Ltd., Padstow, Cornwall

This book is printed on acid-free paper

1

It was early evening as Zoe Carson breasted a hill top and saw before her the sea, smooth and blue, reaching out to meet the sky. The road wound down again towards the seashore and far below she could see the rooftops of the village and the stalwart tower of the grey stone church drowsing in the evening sun. There was a small harbour and most of the houses huddled round it, or climbed the hillside that rose behind, straggling upward and staring out across the sea, as if watching for the return of the fishing boats.

Port Marsden was built in a fold in the hill and the cliffs rose steeply on either side, spreading away deceptively smooth and green. There were a few houses above the village bordering a coast road, standing out bravely against the weather. Some had the scant protection of a few trees, but most stood alone, spaced out like sentinels along the cliff.

'Oh, Barney, it's beautiful,' breathed Zoe to the dog at her side. She drew into the gateway of a field and got out of the car. Standing on one of the rungs of the gate she gazed down at the sleeping village below.

'I hope the cottage is near the harbour, don't you?'

Barney, pleased to be out of the car again, was investigating a ditch and the hedgerow with enthusiasm. He did not mind where they were going provided he was included.

With growing excitement Zoe got back into the car and drove down the steep winding hill into the village and pulled up beside the harbour. She had no idea where the cottage was, she had been given no direction or street name, so she crossed over into a little newsagent's opposite the harbour wall which, surprisingly was still open and asked her way. The woman behind the counter peered at her.

'Shearwater Cottage you said? Miss Carson's place?'

'Yes, I'm her niece.' Zoe thought that somehow an explanation seemed necessary.

'I didn't know she had a niece,' said the woman.

'I didn't know I had an aunt,' said Zoe smiling. 'Could you direct me, please?'

'Of course, my dear. Take the cliff road out of the village and up the hill a way. On the left you'll pass some stone gateposts, they're the drive to Shearwater House and if you go a little further, on the right, you'll see the cottage. It's got two apple trees in the garden. You can't miss it.'

'Thank you very much,' said Zoe. 'I'll find it, I'm sure.'

'Well, if you do have any trouble come back and ask. I'm Mrs. Charter, I've lived here all my life. Anything you want to know, you come and ask me.'

Zoe thanked her again and following

3

the directions, drove through the village and out along the cliff road. Mrs. Charter's directions were good and in minutes she was turning on to the track leading to the cottage. Zoe stopped the car by the dry stone wall and climbed out for her first look at Shearwater Cottage, the cottage her unknown aunt had left her.

It was not at all as she had imagined it, sitting in her backyard in London; no pink-washed walls or roses round the door, no thatched roof and sheltered garden. It stood stark and bleak on the cliff top. Built of hard grey stone with a roof of grey slate, it had a stubby chimney at each end. The windows were small and peered out anxiously from under gables; the door, sheltered by a small porch was heavy solid oak with a huge black knocker. As Zoe regarded the cottage solemnly, the first piece of property she had owned, it seemed to crouch lower and look at the same time forlorn and forbidding.

Calling Barney who was already

exploring the smells in the garden and the lane, Zoe went up to the front door and selecting one of the keys on the ring the solicitor had given her, tried the door. It opened smoothly enough and with Barney at her heels Zoe stepped into the coolness of the house.

She found she was in the living room, as wide as the cottage with windows facing both the sea and the garden. These were curtained and Zoe immediately crossed over and threw back the drapes. As the evening sun flooded into the room and Zoe could see it properly, she felt her spirits lift. It was a square room with a fireplace at one end and full of heavy old furniture. There was a sideboard along one wall, once lovingly polished though now its shine was dulled by a film of dust, and it was covered with china figurines. There was a rocking chair beside the empty fireplace and a half-empty log box opposite. A table and chairs stood under one seaward window and there was a window seat under the other.

Immediately opposite the front door were two more doors, both closed. One led to the kitchen and the other revealed the staircase, steep and narrow, leading to the rooms above. The stairs were uncarpeted and Barney rushed up them ahead of Zoe, slithering and clicking with his claws as he did so.

There were three rooms upstairs. One was as big as the living room; its windows looked out to sea from under the little slated gables, and its ceiling sloped almost to the floor on that side. The other two rooms had been converted from one large one, making a tiny bedroom looking back across the cliff and a bathroom with a window facing out to sea. The rooms were still furnished with Aunt Jessie's things. Her clothes hung in the wardrobe, her china decorated the kitchen dresser, even her book lay unfinished by her white-quilted bed. Zoe felt a surge of sadness for her unknown aunt. In a strange way she felt as if she were intruding, as if she had no right to be there, about to use the everyday things her aunt had left behind.

'But that's silly,' she said to Barney, 'because she wanted me to have them or she wouldn't have left them to me.' All the same Zoe decided to sleep in the little bedroom, not to disturb the quiet peace of her aunt's room. She collected her luggage from the Mini and parked the car in the space beside the house. Then, having unrolled her sleeping bag on the spare bed and put Barney's blanket in one corner of the room, Zoe decided to eat, and unpacked the box of food she had brought with her. She hunted in the kitchen cupboards for a frying pan and a saucepan and soon had a plate of bacon and eggs and a cup of coffee. She carried them through to the living room and ate her supper seated at the table in the window, looking out across the cliff top to the sea beyond. The silence and the stillness were complete.

The dusk turned to darkness and Zoe switched on the lights before going into the kitchen to wash up. She busied herself putting the food away in the old pantry and discovered a store cupboard full of tins and some battered looking packets of soups and cereal. There was a door opposite the back door which was locked, and intrigued, Zoe got out Aunt Jessie's ring of keys to see if one of them would open it. There was a large key which looked the right shape and sure enough it slipped into the keyhole and the lock turned. The door opened inwards, straight on to the top of a flight of stairs; it was the door to the cellar. Zoe looked for a light switch, but could not find one. The darkness was complete and so she decided not to venture down the steps until she had daylight to help her; even Barney seemed disinclined to explore down in that cold blackness and after one sniff at the top of the stone steps scuttled back to the light warmth of the kitchen.

'We'll explore properly tomorrow, Barney,' said Zoe, and they were both content with that.

Zoe was about to climb the steep stairs to her bed when the silence was shattered by a loud banging on the front door. The noise was so loud and so sudden that Zoe nearly cried out in fright and Barney barked furiously, jumping in vertical leaps in his excitement. Cautiously Zoe opened the heavy door and Barney rushed out into the darkness, still barking.

'Steady on, old chap. Good dog! Down, dog!' said a man's voice. 'It's all right, I'm a friend, I'm a friend,' and into the shaft of light thrown by the open door stepped a tall man, his hands spread out to fend off the still barking dog.

'Who are you?' asked Zoe, making no move to catch Barney until the visitor had established his identity.

'James Penrose,' came the reply. 'I live at Shearwater House. Can you do something about your dog? I'm sure he's only doing his job but I can't get through the door.'

Zoe was still not sure she wanted the

stranger inside the door at half past ten at night, but she said, 'Barney, stop it. Come here.' Barney came reluctantly to her side, and stood poised to renew his attack should he deem it necessary.

'I live at Shearwater House,' repeated the man, 'and when we saw the lights on here we thought I'd better come over and see who was here. We know the cottage should be empty, so you'll excuse me asking who you are and what you're doing.'

'I'm Zoe Carson, my aunt left me the cottage in her will and I've come down to look at it.'

'Oh, I see. I'm sorry to have troubled you so late, but we were afraid it might be squatters, students or something, making use of an empty house.'

'How very kind of you to take the trouble,' said Zoe warmly. 'I'm sorry, do come inside for a moment. Barney, stay!' and she stood aside to let James Penrose into the cottage.

He crossed the threshold and walked with assurance into the living room as if he were used to doing so and was at home there. He perched on the arm of a chair and looked quizzically at Zoe.

'So you're Miss Carson's niece. She must have been your great-aunt.'

'She was,' said Zoe. 'My father's aunt.'

'You never came to see her when she was alive.' James Penrose was not accusing, he merely stated it as a fact.

'No.' Zoe felt her reply needed some amplification and added, 'I didn't know she existed. My father died when I was very young and we lost touch with his family.'

'And now you've come down to look the place over.' Again it was not a question, just a statement of fact, as if he had made several deductions already and was mentally checking them out and crossing them off in his mind. He glanced round the room.

'It's a nice room this, I've always liked it; cosy and comfortable yet dignified, if you see what I mean.' Zoe did see what he meant, she had already made a similar judgement and was using it to help draw a mental picture of her unknown aunt.

'You'll sell, of course?' This time there was a query in his voice.

'Oh, yes,' said Zoe. 'I live and work in London. It's too far for a weekend cottage and I couldn't live down here.'

He nodded, his eyes fixed for a moment on her face. Although she could feel the colour rising in her cheeks she held his gaze.

'Well,' he said, 'I won't disturb you any more. I hope you didn't mind my coming over. We always kept an eye on the place for your aunt, you know, if she was away, kept a spare key in case she locked herself out or something. I hope I didn't frighten you.'

'No, not at all,' said Zoe seeing him to the door. 'I'm grateful that you took the trouble.' She paused with her hand on the door handle and then said, 'Did you know my aunt well?'

'Quite well, though my mother knew her better.' He seemed to understand that she wanted to know more and added, 'Now we're neighbours, if only for a short while, you must come over and meet my mother. She'd love to meet you and she could tell you far more about your aunt than I can.'

Zoe thanked him. 'I'm only here for the weekend this time,' she said, 'but I'll be coming to Cornwall again to arrange the sale and sort out what's here.'

'Then we'll certainly meet again. You must come over for a meal next time you're here.' He eased himself past her and stood for a moment on the step.

'Goodnight, Miss Carson. It's been a pleasure to meet you.'

'Goodnight, Mr. Penrose. So kind of you to come over.'

Zoe closed the door and wondered; their parting had been so formal. She went back slowly and dropped into the rocking chair. Barney jumped up on to her knee and she stroked him absent-mindedly.

'What a strange man, Barney,' she mused. 'There was definitely something forceful about him, didn't you think? But did he really come over prepared to repel boarders?'

As she considered her late night caller, Zoe found that in some peculiar way he seemed to grow in stature. Admittedly he was tall, but somehow in her mind he seemed to tower over her. His eyes were dark, yet in her mental image of him they smouldered with a strange energy. He must have been in his late thirties but in recollection his age seemed indefinable. There was something about him that intrigued Zoe, though she had not warmed to him instinctively as she did to so many people.

'Your trouble is that you accept everyone at face value,' her mother had once said, and she knew it was true; she expected people to be as they seemed and once she had accepted a person as one thing she found it difficult to revise her opinion. But James Penrose did not fit into any convenient category, and in a strange way she found him disturbing, his eyes were so penetrating, boring into her and seeming to read her thoughts, she was glad she had nothing to hide from him.

'I wonder what Robert would make of him, Barney,' wondered Zoe as she switched off the lights and they climbed the stairs to the tiny bedroom under the eaves. Barney snuffled about and settled himself in his corner of the room, unconcerned by the question.

'You're probably right,' agreed Zoe as she slipped into her sleeping bag. 'The question will never arise.' And thinking comfortably about Robert, she drifted into sleep.

2

Next morning when she awoke, Zoe gazed at the low white ceiling of her room and wondered for a moment where she was. Immediately she was fully awake she realised that she was in her own cottage, Shearwater Cottage, on a cliff in Cornwall and to prove it she could hear the waves pounding on the beach at the foot of that cliff. She sat up in bed and at once Barney stirred in his corner and padded across the room to her side.

'Well, Barney,' she announced, 'we're here, and I think it's time to get up.'

She was soon down in the kitchen making toast for breakfast and longing to explore the village and its surrounding countryside. As soon as she opened the back door, Barney had set off on his own voyage of exploration and Zoe found herself wanting to follow him out

16

into the summer sun. Although she knew there was plenty of sorting out to be done on the house, she felt the pull of the warm June day and allowed herself to be tempted out to enjoy it, with the need to buy more food from the village as her excuse.

Whistling to Barney, she set off to walk to Port Marsden for some supplies. Her first stop was Mrs. Charter's newsagent's. Mrs. Charter greeted her like a long-lost friend and with an air of great superiority, introduced her to other customers in the shop.

'You won't have met Miss Carson yet, I expect. The new Miss Carson living up at Shearwater Cottage.' She spoke with a proprietorial air as if she owned Zoe and was displaying her with pride.

Thus, Zoe met the village and several minutes later escaped thankfully from Mrs. Charter, to explore in peace the little winding streets, the harbour and little square beside the harbour wall.

With Barney beside her she sat on that wall and watched the fishing boats leave on the tide, allowing the gentle peace of the place to envelop her.

It's great to visit, she thought, her thoughts ringing loud and clear in her head as always, but I wouldn't want to live here.

'Miss Carson!' Her reveries were interrupted by the clipped voice of James Penrose, her late-night visitor. 'I don't think you know my mother.' Without further ado he introduced an elderly woman whose only concession to age was her grey hair. She was small and bright-eyed, her eyes darting from place to place, missing nothing and giving Zoe the impression that not only was nothing missed now, but that nothing would be forgotten later. She felt Mrs. Penrose studying her, noting her faded jeans and comfortable shirt, and she was glad Barney was sitting decorously at her feet and not creating the din he had the previous night when James Penrose had knocked at the door.

18

'I'm so glad to meet you,' said Mrs. Penrose, her hand extended in greeting. 'I knew your aunt well, and though she never discussed her family, I'm sure she'd be glad the cottage was not neglected. She loved it herself, and wouldn't move down into the village even though she found shopping difficult.'

Zoe tried to say all the right things, but with no knowledge of her aunt beyond that which she had managed to glean from the house itself, she felt rather at a loss. Mrs. Penrose seemed unperturbed by Zoe's non-committal answers and declared that certainly she must come for dinner next time she was down and if there was anything of Aunt Jessie's for which Zoe had no use, clothes and such, the dear vicar would no doubt be delighted to take them off her hands.

A little overwhelmed by the barrage of conversation, Zoe agreed to go to dinner next time she was in Port Marsden and made her escape from the

Penroses with pleas of pressure of work at the cottage. But as she approached Shearwater Cottage once more, meandering slowly along the lane with Barney enjoying himself immensely in the hedgerows, she felt less and less like sorting the cupboards, sifting through the contents which had belonged to her aunt.

'But if I don't, Barney, it'll all be waiting next time I come, so I'd better make a start.'

After lunch Zoe settled down to going through Aunt Jessie's things and became so involved with what she found that she discovered it was early evening before she really noticed that the time had passed, and it was only Barney's restlessness which made her realise how late it was.

'All right, dog,' she said, getting up stiffly from the floor where she had been examining a drawer of faded photographs. 'We'll go for a walk before supper.' And closing the back door behind her, Zoe led the way out along the track to the lane.

'Come on, Barney,' she called cheerfully, glad now that she was out of the house again, to be away from the smell of dust and age.

They set off along the little road, but this time away from the village, following its twists and turns across the cliff top. The hedgerows, spangled with wild flowers, gleamed with unexpected colour in the evening sun, and the scent of summer hung in the air, spiced by the faint sea breeze. Everything was still and a gentle lethargy rested there. The peace was suddenly and rudely broken by the roaring of a car coming up some hidden hill and sweeping round the corner in the middle of the road at a speed which caused the tyres to squeal in protest. Zoe leapt for the shelter of the hedge and Barney, who had been happily investigating the smells in the grass verge on the opposite side of the lane, made a dash for safety at his mistress's side. His sudden emergence from the long grass made the car, an open-topped MGB, swerve violently to avoid him and run up on to the grass bank where it stopped. There was a short-lived, uncomfortable silence, while Zoe, too shocked to move, cowered into the hedge and Barney whimpered untouched, but terrified, at her feet, then the driver of the car erupted from his seat and without opening his car door swung his long legs over the side and strode across to Zoe, his eyes blazing with rage.

'Don't you know better than to have your dog out of control in a country lane? It could have caused a major accident, hurtling across the road like that.'

Zoe felt a flame of anger, which matched his, flare up inside her.

'You're a fine one to talk about accidents,' she retorted. 'If I'd been in a car coming the other way there'd have been a head-on collision, the speed you were travelling, and on the wrong side of the road. You should be had up for dangerous driving.' She stared up at him defiantly and encountered the most brilliant blue eyes she had ever seen, flashing with anger now, but with the creases of laughter at their corners. His hair was an unruly thatch of blond straw, made even more disordered by his speed in the open car. Zoe, absurdly aware of her faded jeans and checked shirt, felt suddenly at a disadvantage and bending down picked up the still-whining Barney. From the safety of her arms he faced the angry man more bravely and began to bark.

Turning abruptly on his heel, and without saying another word, the driver of the car got back into the driving seat and loudly revving the engine, backed the red sports car off the grass verge and continued his journey towards the village.

'Maniac,' said Zoe to Barney as she set him down again, though she had to admit on looking at the sharp corner again that it would have been difficult to come round it without taking up most of the road because the lane was so narrow.

Within the next hundred yards Zoe

found a footpath which left the road and broke across the cliff at right angles, leading through the coarse grass to within feet of the cliff edge before turning to wander along the undulating coastline. The evening was so beautiful that Zoe followed the winding track across the cliffs, pausing from time to time to peer cautiously down into the tiny coves below. Occasionally these had narrow paths zig-zagging down to the beach, but others had sheer drops and one carried a warning about the danger of a rockfall and she drew fearfully back from the edge. At last hunger made her turn, and they followed the cliff track right back to Shearwater Cottage. Indeed the path appeared to go beyond and Zoe assumed it wound all the way down into Port Marsden.

Zoe breakfasted leisurely next morning and then decided to attend service at the little grey stone church in the village. She had noticed yesterday that it was at eleven o'clock, and hoping the vicar would not object to her jeans and shirt which were all she had with her, she shut Barney into the car and set off along the cliff path to the village. As she had predicted, it led down through some steep twisting back lanes into the main square by the harbour, and from there it was only a step to the church of St Michael perched on a rise beyond the shops. The bells were ringing out from the tower and Zoe joined the last one or two who scurried up the slope and in through the great oak door at the west end.

After the service, as everyone filed out shaking hands with the vicar, Zoe felt a hand on her arm and turned to find Mrs. Penrose, resplendent in her Sunday hat, beaming at her.

'My dear, how lovely to see you in church. Do let me introduce you to the dear vicar, such a charming man.' And before Zoe could protest, Mrs. Penrose propelled her to the church porch and introduced her to Mr. Campion, the vicar.

'Miss Carson's niece, Zoe, Vicar. Come to see Shearwater Cottage and sort everything out.'

The vicar smiled at Zoe and taking her hand said, 'How nice to welcome you to our church, Zoe. We're always delighted to see new faces amongst the familiar ones.' Zoe warmed to him at once and returned his smile.

'I expect you'd like to visit your aunt's grave if you haven't already,' he said. 'If you like to wait for a moment I'll show you where it is.'

'Thank you,' said Zoe, 'I'll wait outside.'

'I'll show her, Vicar,' beamed Mrs. Penrose, determined to be included.

'Thank you, Mrs. Penrose,' replied the vicar courteously. 'I'll join you in a moment or two.' Mrs. Penrose piloted Zoe across the neat little churchyard towards the grey stone wall that encircled it.

There in a corner shaded by an age-old yew tree, was a simple grey slab with Aunt Jessie's name and the dates of her life carved into it. Zoe stood for a minute looking down at it and she thought, Thank you, Aunt Jessie, for remembering me. I'm sorry I've got to sell your cottage, because I'm fond of it already, but my life isn't here, it's in London, and a whispered thought came unbidden, with Robert, but she disregarded it. In the silence of the churchyard Zoe tried to feel something more than interest for her unknown aunt, but that silence was rudely shattered by the roar of a car engine and she glanced up sharply to see a red MGB pulling away noisily from the harbour square and disappearing up the hill out of the village.

The vicar crossed over to where she stood and immediately Mrs. Penrose reclaimed her proprietorial rights and insinuated herself between them so that she should be included in their conversation.

'James will be picking me up in a moment or two, do let us save you a walk up the hill Zoe. I may call you

Zoe, mayn't I?' and taking permission for granted she continued without pause, 'And we'll drop you at the cottage. Your aunt found that hill a trial towards the end. We did what we could, of course, our Christian duty,' she flashed a beatific smile at the patient vicar, 'but she was so independent, wasn't she, Vicar?' The vicar agreed and then added, 'I think I can see your son's car waiting, Mrs. Penrose.'

'So it is,' trilled Mrs. Penrose. 'Come along, Zoe, we must go.' Mr. Campion smiled at Zoe and once more took her hand.

'A pleasure to meet you, Zoe. Mrs. Penrose is obviously looking after you very well, but if there's anything I can do at any time, the vicarage is next to the church and my wife and I would love to see you, even if only for a cup of coffee and a chat.'

Zoe thanked him and then found herself being ushered into a shining Jaguar. Mrs. Penrose continued to chatter as they pulled away and when she mentioned the narrowness of the lanes, Zoe told them about the near accident on the cliff top road the previous evening. She did not describe the driver of the car, but at the mention of it being a red MGB Mrs. Penrose sniffed.

'Gregory Enodoc! Always drives too fast.'

Though pressed to join the Penroses for lunch, Zoe felt she had had enough of Mrs. Penrose for one morning and refused gently but firmly, promising to go to dinner next time she was in Port Marsden. She accepted James's card and stood thankfully at the end of the track which led to the cottage to wave them goodbye.

'Don't forget, phone us before you come down and we'll air the cottage and get in a few groceries for you.'

Zoe promised and the car pulled away with Mrs. Penrose's instructions still issuing from the window.

As she walked up the track Zoe glanced at the card. Printed on it were the words: James Penrose Import Export. There was an office address and telephone number in Plymouth and his home address and number at Shearwater House, Port Marsden. She stuffed it into the pocket of her jeans and went to find Barney.

That night, in bed, Zoe thought about her weekend, the cottage, the village and the people she had met. She was not at all sure about James Penrose, she found his direct gaze rather unnerving, almost impertinent as if he could see through her clothes to her skin. Mrs. Penrose meant well, but was a little overpowering. The vicar was, well, the vicar. She thought she would like to know him better and meet his wife, whom Mrs. Penrose had described as 'a slip of a thing but nice enough and works hard'. The throaty roar of a sports car split the night and Zoe felt sure she could put a name to its driver. Gregory Enodoc.

'Though it probably isn't at all,' she said sleepily to Barney, 'there must be hundreds of cars that sound the same.'

The silence surged back round her and with it came the whisper of the sea which seemed to deepen the silence rather than break it. Zoe and Barney slept.

3

The nearer Zoe came to London and her office next day, the more she longed to be there. This was her real world and as the miles clocked up between her and Port Marsden the more unreal the little village became, as if she had dreamed it and the dream was fading in the bright light of day. For a while she tried to hold on to the shreds of it, to conjure up the cottage and the cliff top into clear pictures in her mind, but the images were already blurred, and by the time she had followed the Thames Embankment through the heat and dust to the office building and ducked down into its underground car park, she found she had only the haziest recollections of what Shearwater Cottage and Port Marsden looked like and these were pushed aside by a growing fear that she was late and had missed

Robert's call from New York.

Robert Stackton was the central pillar of Zoe's life. He was her boss, but she was more than his personal assistant; she had been with him as he had gradually built up his company, Amalgamated Chemicals, from a struggling one-man firm into a fast-expanding concern moving into international markets. Zoe loved him blindly; concealing her passion from him, yet longing to remove him from the clinically efficient office environment so that he would see her in a different light and his casual affection for her might be transformed to something stronger. Deep within her, Zoe treasured dreams of Robert suddenly realising how much he loved her and whirling her off her feet into a passionate embrace. When facing reality she was more practical; she tried to be everything he needed so that she became an indispensible part of his life.

Zoe had been bitterly disappointed when he had taken Mr. Paterson and Mr. Paterson's secretary, Rosemary, to

America on his latest business trip; he had half promised that she should go the next time and Zoe had regarded the trip as the opportunity she had been waiting for to alter and develop her relationship with Robert. He had softened her disappointment a little by telling her he needed her to run the London office, but she missed him sorely, as she always did while he was away, particularly this time as the man-eating Rosemary was with him. The part Mr. Paterson might play as a chaperone was of no consolation to Zoe at all, but once she had come to terms with her disappointment and jealousy, Zoe threw herself whole-heartedly into her work to ease the passing of time until Robert was home again.

It had been Robert's suggestion during his last call from New York that Zoe should get out of London for a long weekend, and acting upon it, Zoe had taken the chance to go and see the cottage her great-aunt had left her. In the cool greenness of Port Marsden she had forgotten the dusty bustle of her London life for a few days, and strangely enough even Robert hardly troubled her thoughts; but now with Cornwall forgotten in its turn, she hurried up to her office to wait for his call, longing to hear his voice even if only over a crackling line from New York. The interlude was over and life as she had come to live it returned, and she started to open the mail.

When the call finally came through Robert sounded on top of the world.

'The panic's over,' he cried. 'Everything seems to be sorting itself out. Hope to be back by the end of the week. All right your end?'

Zoe said it was.

'Good. All the news on Friday then. Goodbye.'

The days until Friday dragged by. Robert phoned once more to tell her his arrival time, but in his absence Zoe gradually became aware that it was not her actual job which was so exciting, but working for Robert Stackton; when all things were considered much of her work was pretty routine, what made it exciting was working for Robert, coming in every day to find him sitting at his desk or pacing his office and being a sort of partner in his worries and his triumphs. She was not involved emotionally with her job, only her boss.

When he finally sauntered into the office on Friday afternoon, Zoe longed to rush to him and feel his arms fold round her in welcome.

Oh, Robert, she cried out in her mind, I've missed you so. But all she did was stand up to receive his brief case and say, 'Good journey back?'

Robert nodded. 'Yes, thanks, I've sent Rosemary and Mr. Paterson home until Monday to catch up on their jet-lag.' He laughed and Zoe found her jealousy for Rosemary warring with the thrill his laughter gave her.

'Now we seem to have sorted out the New York end for the time being, what's been going on here?'

They spent the rest of the afternoon

and early evening closeted together as Robert Stackton caught up on the day to day business he had missed while he was away; then leaning back in his chair and swivelling it round to look out across the twilight city, Robert said, 'Drink at the Bugle?' Zoe felt her heart jump within her, but outwardly calm she replied, 'Yes, if you're not too tired.' Robert stretched and stood up, snapping his brief case shut as he did so. 'Just a quickie then,' and they adjourned to the pub next door.

They took their drinks out on to the terrace to enjoy the last of the evening warmth.

'Well,' said Robert taking a long pull at his very large whisky, 'how was this famous cottage then?' So Zoe told him, and far from the brief description she had intended, she found herself describing the place in detail, trying to recreate for Robert how she had first seen Port Marsden peacefully mellow in the evening sun, and the strange sturdiness of the little cottage hugging the cliff top; and as she spoke she found she could now see again, with startling clarity, the view from the cottage windows and the quiet strength of the grey stone church. Once speaking she felt unable to stop, she had had no one to share her thoughts and ideas with, and as Robert sat in the growing dusk listening to her, she told him of the hedgerows and the rolling cliffs, of James Penrose and his mother, of the quiet simple grave under the yew tree in the churchyard. When finally she lapsed into silence all Robert said was, 'Sounds nice. Who was this Penrose chap? What does he do?'

'I don't know,' said Zoe flatly, suddenly disappointed at Robert's lack of interest in Shearwater and Port Marsden. 'His card said something about Import/Export.'

'Sounds impressive, you ought to cultivate him.' And with those few words Robert caused Zoe to regret how she had spoken of Port Marsden; she felt strangely empty inside as if everything was spoilt, but completely unaware of her feelings, Robert continued, 'You'll have to go down again to arrange the sale of the place. I expect your friend James would be only too pleased to help you. He seems keen to pursue the friendship.'

'Well, I will,' Zoe said. 'I thought I'd take a couple of weeks of my holiday when it's convenient.'

'Anytime you like. Now the panic in America is over, we should be fairly quiet. You've kept this end ticking over nicely, so you can go when you like.'

'I'll go next week then,' said Zoe, without enthusiasm. 'I'll go down and sort it all out before the autumn.'

'Right,' said Robert downing his drink. 'Well, I'll see you on Monday and you can take off next weekend.' He stood up to go.

'Coming?'

'No,' said Zoe. 'I haven't finished my drink yet. I'll enjoy the peace for a few minutes more.' In a strange detached way she watched her boss walk away from her and knew that whatever had or had not happened in New York, there was a subtle difference in their relationship. Something had changed and she felt as if Robert Stackton had walked away from her for ever. Her thoughts were interrupted by the revving of a sports car in the street beyond the terrace wall and for a moment she remembered the handsome face of Gregory Enodoc before she sighed and started for home.

Whether it was because Robert had told her to cultivate James Penrose or whether it was her own reticence, Zoe was not sure, but she did not telephone ahead to warn the Penroses of her arrival on the next Sunday. Having cleared up the flat and packed far more into the Mini than last time, Zoe bundled Barney on to the passenger seat and spent Sunday driving comfortably down to Port Marsden. Breasting the hill above the village she paused to look down on its roofs, straggling in the fold of the cliffs and felt a sudden wave of pleasure sweep through her.

'Come on, Barney,' she said, letting in the clutch, 'let's get a move on.' The radio was chattering away quietly to itself and hoping to hear the weather forecast, Zoe turned it up as the pips went. The news came first and Zoe had to listen to tales of rising unemployment, strikes, a prisoner escaped from Dartmoor and the dangers of forest fires in the West of England.

'What a depressing five minutes!' she remarked to Barney as she switched off thankfully after hearing warnings of storms along the south coast. 'Strikes and prisoners and storms. We won't have that radio on again until we go home. The world can get on without us.'

Shearwater Cottage was as she had left it, but somehow this time she felt welcomed by its grey walls and peering windows; it was as if it had been watching for her, and she and Barney slipped happily into its peaceful silence. The quiet of the evening was soon disturbed though by the gentle rumble of thunder; gradually the air was filled with curls of stormy darkness as louring clouds built up. The sun vanished and a chilly wind sprang up, sweeping across the cliff top making the back door bang and the open windows rattle.

Zoe hurried round the house closing the windows she had earlier opened to let in the fresh sea air. She always enjoyed a thunder storm from the safe warmth of her home and so she settled down in the unlit living room to watch it break over the sea. The sky was split by a sudden flash of lightning and the patter of huge raindrops echoed on the roof, gradually increasing to a steady drumming on the slates. The rain lashed against the windows curtaining them with grey water. All around the thunder rumbled, grumbling to itself before exploding into a vicious crack right overhead, with simultaneous lightning jagging the storm-torn sky. It was one of the most spectacular storms Zoe had ever seen, and caught in the curving coastline, it raged for more than an hour before it began to drift away, with only the odd rumble of thunder and the drenched landscape to mark its passing. It was quite dark now and Zoe crept upstairs to the bed waiting invitingly in the small bedroom.

The next morning she woke to a clear, bright day with the last vestiges of the storm vanished. Zoe thought she would visit the estate agent. She had seen one in a tiny timbered office down on the harbour square and decided, despite Robert's insistence that she use a big firm in Truro or Plymouth, to go first to Grant, Pollard & Co., to see what they thought about the cottage.

When she had tidied away the breakfast things she left Barney in the car, where he was always happiest if left alone, and set off down the path to the village. The cold wind which had arisen with the storm had gone and the sun struck warm across her shoulders as she followed the track down into the narrow lanes and out into the harbour square. She looked round for the old sign she had seen the previous evening as she drove through the village on her way to Shearwater and found it in neat black Gothic lettering above the bow-window of a small white house.

She crossed over and looked into the window, to see the cards and pictures advertising property for sale. There seemed to be a wide variety, both in price and type of houses, so she pushed open the studded wooden door and went in.

For a moment Zoe could see nothing for the office was dim and cool after the bright heat of the morning outside, and she was aware only of a tall man standing talking to a girl sitting behind a desk, but as her eyes adjusted to the room she found herself staring into a pair of eyes so brilliantly blue that she recognised them at once. Last time she had seen them they had blazed anger from their depths, now they gazed back at her evenly for a fraction of a second before they reflected the recognition which had jumped to her own. It was Gregory Enodoc.

He took a step forward, and said coolly, 'Good morning. Can I help you?' Zoe took a moment to overcome her surprise and then replied equally coolly, 'I don't know. I'm going to sell my house.'

He nodded. 'I see, well perhaps you'd care to come through to my office.' The words were civil enough, but Zoe felt an underlying arrogance in his manner and was irritated that her insistence on using a local agent had led her to dealing with Gregory Enodoc.

'Well,' she hesitated, wondering if it was too late to back out and take Robert's advice and go to Truro, but she was forestalled by Gregory Enodoc turning to his secretary and saying, 'No calls while Miss Carson's with me, Jean.' He pushed open a door and stood aside for Zoe to precede him into his office.

'Sit down,' he invited pulling forward

a chair, and Zoe did so.

'How do you know my name?' she asked abruptly.

'My dear girl,' he drawled, 'everyone in Port Marsden knows your name, rest assured, and your business, too, if Mrs. Charter saw you coming in here this morning.'

Zoe flushed warmly and said, 'So you listen to village gossip.' He remained ungoaded and said, 'In a place like this it's as reliable as a newspaper and often far more entertaining.' He smiled and looked suddenly much younger. 'Even our first encounter did not go unre-marked, I've heard of it from several people. Of course I haven't told anyone so perhaps you let something slip in chat ... unless there was someone hiding in the hedge at the time.' Zoe felt angry that she could not deny having told Mrs. Penrose of the incident, but was a little mollified when Gregory said, 'Shall we start again?' and solemnly standing up, extended his hand and spoke as if they had never met before.

'How do you do, Miss Carson, I'm Gregory Enodoc. How nice that you've come to live in Port Marsden.'

Zoe found herself responding to the twinkle in his eyes and taking his hand, smiled back.

'Good,' he said and sat down again. 'Now to business — do you really want to sell Shearwater Cottage?'

'Yes,' nodded Zoe. 'I must. I can't live here and — '

'Why not?' interrupted Gregory.

Zoe stared at him. 'Why not what?'

'Why can't you live here?'

'Well, because I can't. Because I've a job in London that I enjoy and a flat . . . ' her voice trailed away.

'And a man?'

'I beg your pardon?' said Zoe, startled.

'Granted,' replied Gregory unperturbed, 'I said 'and a man?''

'I don't see that is any concern of yours, Mr. Enodoc,' Zoe said sharply.

'No, of course not,' said he soothingly. 'Don't let's quarrel again.' Then
he added, 'My friends call me Greg.'

'Do they?' Zoe spoke with indiffer-
ence.

'Come on Zoe, pax? I won't ask any
more questions.'

Slightly pacified, Zoe smiled. 'All
right. Now the cottage and furniture
must be sold and I want an opinion as
to the price I can ask.'

Greg nodded and drawing a sheet
of paper towards him began to make
notes. When Zoe had explained
exactly what she planned to do about
Shearwater Cottage, Greg said, 'Well
the best thing is for me to come up
and have a look. I know the property
from the outside of course, but I
must see the inside and perhaps give
you some idea what the furniture you
want to sell might fetch in the sale
room.'

Zoe thanked him and added, 'The
sooner the better really, because I
shan't be down here for very long,

and I do want all the arrangements set in motion before I go back up to London.'

Greg promised to come out that afternoon if possible and if not, the next. Minutes later Zoe left the agents' pleased to have got things moving.

4

Zoe retraced her steps up the narrow streets that led to the cliff path. When she emerged on the cliff top she saw a great deal of activity beyond Shearwater Cottage where the cliff dipped and curved away before jutting out to shelter a small bay. Leaving her shopping in her garden, she walked on to investigate. As she approached she could see a police car and several men moving about with ropes and posts. A small group of bystanders had gathered and Zoe joined these, peering to see what had happened.

'Has always been a dangerous patch of cliff, that,' said one man.

'They say the whole footpath's gone,' said another.

'What's happened?' ventured Zoe to the first man. He turned and smiled.

'Landslide. In the storm last night.

Slid right down to the beach. You a visitor?' he inquired. 'Down on holiday, I daresay.'

'Well, new to Port Marsden anyway,' admitted Zoe.

'There was a path here, right down to the cove, zig-zag all the way and near the top was a great overhanging boulder. Seems that loosened and rolled in the storm and took half the cliff with it. They're afraid the whole cliff will go, like last year further round the coast.'

'And that's why they're roping it off,' added the other man. Zoe nodded and watched for a moment as one of the policemen posted notices warning of the danger; then she heard a voice she recognised and turned to find James Penrose standing immediately behind her. His eyes widened in surprise as he realised who she was and a strange expression fleeted across his face before he extended his hand and said, 'Miss Carson, Zoe, I didn't know you were here. Are you back at the cottage? You should have warned us you were coming and we'd have made ready for you. My mother was determined that all should be more comfortable next time you came down.'

Zoe thanked him for the kind thoughts and then added, 'I'll be here for a couple of weeks, perhaps I could call on your mother.'

'A couple of weeks,' repeated James thoughtfully. 'As long as that. How nice,' he went on hastily, 'yes, indeed visit mother, and take us up on our dinner invitation.' He glanced back at the roped off area of cliff. 'Completely collapsed, I hear. Is that true? Were you here last night, did you hear anything?'

'Well, I heard the storm of course, and the thunder was tremendously loud at times, but I can't say I heard the cliff fall. I expect I did but I took it for thunder.'

'Probably,' agreed James. He looked past her and saw one of the policemen coming towards the group. 'Excuse me, I'd just like a word with the sergeant.'

He strode off to speak to the man.

Deciding there was little else to see, Zoe made her way back to the cottage, collected her shopping and let out an ecstatic Barney, who bounced round her in his delight at seeing her again. She switched on the radio while she made herself a sandwich for lunch, to hear the announcer saying ' . . . who escaped from Dartmoor prison yesterday is still at large. In his escape he shot and wounded a prison officer and is himself believed to be wounded. Police warn — ' but Zoe, remembering her promise to herself of no depressing news during her holiday, snapped it off and turned her attention to how she was going to dispose of Aunt Jessie's things; which were to be sold and which to be given away.

It was still early afternoon when there was a knock at the door and on opening it, Zoe found Mrs. Penrose beaming on the doorstep. 'My dear, why didn't you let us know you were coming? We'd have at least got some food in for you.'

She sailed in through the door and deposited herself in the living room. Hardly pausing for breath she continued, 'James tells me you were alone here in the storm last night. My poor girl, what a terrifying experience that must have been! You're so cut off here in this cottage, so far from help if something goes wrong. We're the nearest and we're a quarter of a mile at least. I do hope you don't become nervous all alone. I always fancy I hear noises about the place when I'm by myself at night, and last night with all that thunder and lightning, well, James was out somewhere and I was on my own in the house, too, for a while. I tell you, I was petrified, absolutely petrified. What if the chimney was struck? James says it won't be because of the conductor, but you can't be sure can you?'

Zoe tried to speak, but before she had said more than 'I didn't mind, I rather like . . . ' Mrs. Penrose had interrupted her.

'Now, I know you'll be busy while you're here, but you must have some holiday, too, so I've come to invite you to tea.'

'Tea?' said Zoe. 'When?'

'Now, my dear, this afternoon. Just pick up your bag and come.'

'I'm awfully sorry,' began Zoe, 'but I can't, you see . . .'

'Can't?' exclaimed Mrs. Penrose. 'What nonsense, my dear, of course you can. You can go on working here tomorrow.'

'No,' repeated Zoe firmly. 'I'm sorry, but I have the estate agent coming this afternoon; we're going to decide on a price for the house.'

'Well, give him a call and tell him to come tomorrow. James will be so disappointed if you don't come today.'

'I haven't a phone here,' pointed out Zoe, 'and anyway . . .'

'Nor you have,' cried Mrs. Penrose. 'That's why I had to come over, how silly of me! Never mind, you can ring from our house. Don't worry, the agent won't mind.' Mrs. Penrose was so pressing, as if she would take it as a personal affront if she refused again that Zoe was on the point of accepting the invitation when another knock sounded on the front door. It was Gregory Enodoc.

Zoe was so relieved to see him that she greeted him with a wide smile and invited him in. Seeing that she was not alone and recognising the visitor, Gregory crossed to where the old lady sat and extending his hand said, 'Mrs. Penrose. How are you?'

'Well enough, thank you, Mr. Enodoc,' she replied, but she looked far from pleased to see him. She turned to Zoe and said, 'We're too late to save him a journey, but if you should be finished with your business quickly, don't hesitate to pop over for that cup of tea.'

Zoe thanked her again and saw her to the front door, and it was with relief that she closed it at last on Mrs. Penrose's departing figure.

'Thank goodness you arrived when

you did,' Zoe said as she returned to Greg waiting in the living room.

'She can be a bit domineering, can't she?' agreed Greg. 'They've only lived here for about four years, but she likes to know everything that is going on and to have a finger in every pie.'

'Well, I don't suppose I can escape at least one visit there,' said Zoe, 'and they mean very well, always going out of their way to be friendly and helpful.'

Greg grunted. 'Maybe. Anyway, let's forget them; they're foreigners here. Let's have a look at this house of yours.'

They started upstairs and Greg inspected each room, making notes as to size and facilities; then they came down and did the same in the living room and kitchen.

'What's that?' asked Greg, pointing to the door opposite the back door.

'That's the cellar,' Zoe replied. 'I haven't been down there yet.'

'Let's have a look then,' and Greg opened the door. 'Is there a light?'

'I couldn't find one before,' said Zoe.

'That's one of the reasons I didn't go down, but I've brought a torch this time.'

Armed with her little flashlight they descended the stairs. The cellar below was surprisingly dry and warm, though it was large, running the whole length of the house. Zoe swung the torch round piercing the darkness, making the shadows leap on the ceiling and walls. There were one or two boxes, two old cabin trunks and a neat stack of logs piled up against one wall, and at the far end was a huge glass-fronted bookcase, with large drawers making up its base. It was so big it would have dominated any room and probably for that reason alone it had been relegated to the cellar. Greg and Zoe stared at it in wonder.

'How on earth did that get down here?' said Zoe.

'I don't know for certain,' answered Greg, 'but I've a feeling it's in two separate pieces. I'm not sure that the top even belongs to the bottom. It's a secretaire bookcase, probably Queen Anne. My father would know. Look, the top drawer should open into a desk.' He pulled at the handles, but the drawer appeared to be locked.

'Queen Anne!' repeated Zoe excitedly. 'Is it valuable?'

'Could be, I'm not sure. I'm no expert. Why, do you want to sell it?'

'Well, I don't know,' said Zoe, 'I mean, I didn't even know it was here. I'll have to think about it.' A silence fell as they both stared at the enormous piece by the yellow light of the torch. It was broken by a faint scratching noise.

'What was that?' asked Zoe alarmed.

'I don't know, probably a mouse, or a rat.'

'A rat! Let's get out of here.' Zoe beat a hasty retreat to the cheerful sunlight in the kitchen leaving Greg to follow her if he chose.

They sat down at the kitchen table and Greg accepted the cup of tea she made.

'We can sell the cottage with no

problems, I should think; people are always looking for holiday places. We should get a good price if we hold out for one. Depends how much of a hurry you're in to sell.'

Zoe nodded as she drank her tea and munched a biscuit.

'What about the contents; do you think anyone will buy it furnished?'

'They might,' said Greg, 'especially if it is to be a holiday house; but there are one or two pieces which could be quite valuable. I don't know enough about antiques to be sure, so you'd want an expert opinion, but from the various things I've learnt from my father along the way, I'd say you'd be silly to part with them without having them valued. Queen Anne in the cellar for instance, if she's what I think she is, she's worth selling on her own; if you want to sell her, that is.'

'I think I do,' said Zoe. 'I've nowhere to keep her.'

At last, Greg closed his note-book and said casually, 'I suppose you wouldn't like to join me for a drink at the Duck this evening, if you've nothing else planned?' Zoe, who had viewed the evening alone in the cottage with a little nervousness since Mrs. Penrose had talked of being afraid, said she would love to.

'Where is it?' she asked. 'How do I find it?'

'It's down by the harbour, the Duck and Gluepot, but I'll come and fetch you, of course.'

Zoe, who was used to Robert's rather cursory invitations to meet him in a particular pub without thought for her journey either way, was pleased and promised to be ready when he came for her. She was glad she had packed one or two dresses even though she had not expected to go out much on her working holiday. When she had put them in her case she had done so in case Mrs. Penrose kept her promise and invited her to dinner. Now, as she wallowed in her bath, looking out across the cliff through the uncurtained window flung wide to the summer air, she remembered Mrs. Penrose's pressing invitation to tea and wondered idly why today should be so much more important than tomorrow.

The roar of the red MGB announced Greg's arrival and leaving Barney once again comfortably in her car, Zoe stepped out to spend a quiet evening getting to know a new friend.

Gregory smiled at her as he opened the car door and Zoe decided that the evening was going to be a success. It was, too, at least to a certain extent; Zoe loved the little pub which perched on one of the steep slopes leading down to the harbour, its windows staring out across the sea. The flames of the setting sun kindled sparks on the water and made an orange pathway to the shore. The bar itself was small and timbered and smelt of generations of smoke and liquour. The wide fireplace, now filled with dried flowers and grasses, promised huge log fires in the winter and the glasses hanging above the bar winked in the lamplight. Sinking on to the bench seat by the window, Zoe gave a sigh of content and looked across the rim of her glass at Greg Enodoc, liking what she saw. He smiled and asked her about London.

'It's a great place to visit,' he observed as she paused and allowed her thoughts to drift for a moment to the riverside pub and Robert perched on its redbrick wall, 'but I wouldn't like to live there.' Zoe laughed. 'That's the way I feel about here. It's a very pretty village, but it's too far from the centre of things. Nothing much would ever happen here, one day would merge into another completely unrcmarked.'

'Doesn't that happen in London, too?' asked Greg. 'Is every day so startlingly different from every other? Don't tell me you don't slide into such a routine that you can distinguish between the mid-week days.'

'There always seems to be something happening,' countered Zoe.

'Like the cliff collapsing and gale

force winds sweeping the high tide into the market square?'

'Well, I agree, but those were exceptional things, surely?'

'Of course, but you can't say they didn't happen.'

On this subject they agreed to differ and passed on to other things; and though Zoe felt no thrill go through her when Greg helped her with her jacket and gave her a steadying arm in the darkness down the steps to the car, she felt comfortable in his company and was glad she had met him. She enjoyed his ready wit and could feel the warmth of his smile as it curved his mouth and made his blue eyes dance. He had a certain boyishness about him which made him seem years younger than Robert. Robert so cool and so sophisticated, well-dressed and elegant, who never spoke without giving consideration to his words, who never moved without weighing his actions. For a moment Zoe remembered the occasional kiss Robert had placed on her forehead and a shiver passed through her at the recollection.

'Cold?' enquired Greg and pulled a big white sweater from behind the driving seat. 'Put this on, it's often chilly driving at night with the roof down.' Zoe struggled into the sweater and felt an instant warmth flow through her although she knew it was not the cold which had caused her to shiver. Before he started the engine, Greg turned and slipped an arm round her shoulders, pulling Zoe towards him. He turned her face to his and quietly and expertly kissed her lips. For a moment Zoe remained unresisting within the circle of his arms and then she jerked away and ran an agitated hand through her hair, saying as she did so, 'Greg, please don't.'

Greg smiled ruefully. 'Sorry, I'd forgotten. Forbidden territory.' Without further comment he started the car and roared up the coast road towards Shearwater Cottage. He slowed down as he took the track across the cliff and as they drew up beside the cottage they could hear Barney barking. They were walking up to the front door when suddenly, out of the darkness of the front porch, a man barged between them, making Zoe cry out as he sent her flying with his elbow and forced his way clear of Greg's restraining hand, escaping at a run across the cliff. For a moment they heard his feet on the stony track and then he was gone and a strange and unnatural silence fell, broken only by the continued yelping of Barney, locked in the car. Greg helped Zoe to her feet.

'Are you all right?' he asked anxiously. 'Did he hurt you?'

'No, I'm all right,' said Zoe shakily. 'No real damage.' She managed a brave laugh. 'I hope he didn't take anything.'

'We'll soon see,' said Greg quietly, and he took the key from her hand, opened the front door and switched on the lights. Zoe felt her heart pounding as she asked, 'Do you think he was still breaking in?'

'I imagine so, though why he didn't run off as soon as your dog began to bark, I don't know.'

'Perhaps he knew the house was empty. Barney was shut in the car so he wouldn't have been able to go for the burglar.'

Greg looked round the living room, now cheerfully bright with all the lamps on, and said, 'I don't think he'd been inside. It all looks very tidy. Anything missing?'

Zoe, who had let Barney out of the car and was now in the kitchen called out, 'I don't know. I don't really know what was there.' Greg following her into the kitchen, saw that she had a dark red mark coming up on one cheek bone. He crossed to the sink and damping a tea towel in cold water handed it to her.

'Here, put this on your face, it may stop you having a black eye in the morning.' Zoe took the cloth and pressed its coolness to her smarting face, then together they toured the house to see if anything had been disturbed. Back in the living room Greg said, 'Can I get you a drink of something? Have you got any brandy?' Zoe shook her head. Suddenly feeling very tired she sank into one of the fireside chairs. 'No, thank you. I think I'll just go to bed. I'm whacked.'

'I think you should report this to the police,' said Greg.

'I will, in the morning,' said Zoe wearily, 'but I've no phone here and I'm not turning out again tonight.'

'I'll phone from the village if you like.' He hesitated and said, 'I don't like to think of you here alone now. Would you like me to stay? I could easily doss down here.'

'No, thanks all the same,' said Zoe. 'Honestly I'll be all right, and if you call out the police tonight I'll have to wait up for some policeman to come and write it all down. I'm not alone, I've got Barney, so please don't worry. All I want to do now is fall into bed and sleep until morning.'

Reluctantly Greg agreed that the

report could wait until morning, 'But I'm going to call the police first thing,' he said as he took his leave, and with a wave of his hand and the roar of his car, he vanished into the night, leaving Zoe to double check the doors and windows which Greg had already checked, to chain and bolt the front door and to climb the steep stairs to the comfort of her bed.

5

P.C. Dewar arrived at Shearwater Cottage next morning while Zoe was still lingering over her second cup of coffee. He was an elderly man, his fair hair greying so that it had a strange salt and pepper colour and his face creased with lines of worry and laughter. She poured him a cup of coffee and they sat at the table in the window while he solemnly wrote down Zoe's version of the incident the previous night.

'You're sure there was nothing taken, miss?'

Zoe shook her head, 'I can't be sure, because I don't know exactly what ought to be here, but Mr. Enodoc and I think that we interrupted him, whoever it was, before he'd actually got in. The front door was still locked and there were no windows broken or anything. He came out of the porch.'

'You're sure it was a man?'

Zoe looked surprised. 'As sure as I can be,' she said. The constable nodded and made notes in his notebook.

'May I ask, miss, how you came by the black eye?'

'He, the burglar, pushed me over as he got away,' said Zoe. 'It was his elbow, I think.' She touched the bruise gingerly and winced as she did so. The policeman asked a few more general questions and then wandered round the house looking carefully at window catches and door jambs for signs of forced entry.

'Have you ever lost a door key?' he asked as he snapped shut his notebook and prepared to leave, 'or lent one to anybody?'

'I haven't,' said Zoe, 'but of course my aunt may have.'

'I see. Well, if you have any more trouble don't hesitate to let us know. Let that dog of yours roam in the garden at night; he'll warn off a would-be intruder. And one of us'll drive past occasionally during the night. Keep an eye on you.'

Zoe thanked him and closing the door behind him returned to the sunny silence of the living room.

'I really must go round the house and make a catalogue of everything in it,' she told Barney who was sitting expectantly by the back door in the hope of a walk, 'then I can decide exactly what I want to sell and what we'll take up to London,' and armed with a notepad and pencil, she went up the narrow stairs to tackle Aunt Jessie's room.

A faint fragrance of lavender mingled with dust and polish hung in the warm air of that room. Zoe paused in the doorway, allowing the presence of Aunt Jessie to wash over her and then stepped into the bedroom and felt welcome there. She crossed to the windows and threw them open to the morning sun. Zoe inhaled deeply and then set to work. She found a suitcase on top of the wardrobe and into it she carefully packed all her aunt's clothes, saving only a couple of head squares and a sheepskin jacket for herself. Then slowly and methodically she went through the drawers and bedside shelves, throwing out half-used cosmetics, collecting papers and letters into a box to sort out later and dusting the furniture to its well-established gleam.

I think I'll move into this room now, she thought suddenly and so she stripped and remade the bed with clean sheets she had found in the airing cupboard in the bathroom. She unpacked her case into the wardrobe and drawers, set her make-up and hairbrush before the mirror on top of the chest and replaced Aunt Jessie's book on the bedside shelf with the one she was reading. Finally she put out the photograph of Robert which she had cut from a newspaper and framed. She had arrived. The room was hers and looking round at its clean simplicity, sun-warmed and fragrant, she loved it.

Zoe worked steadily through the day, pausing occasionally to brew and drink a cup of coffee before returning to her task and by mid-afternoon she was tired and dustily dishevelled and she welcomed the interruption when there was a knock on the front door. Thinking it was probably Gregory come to see how she was after the incident the night before, she wiped her hands on her apron and threw open the door to let him in. It was not Greg, however, whom she found on the doorstep, but a woman not much older than herself who greeted her with a friendly smile and an extended hand.

'Hallo,' she said, 'I'm Anne Campion, the vicar's wife. You met my husband a couple of Sundays ago.'

'Yes, of course,' said Zoe returning her smile. 'How nice to meet you, do come in.' She led the way into the sitting room and waving her hand at various piles of books and papers on the floor, said, 'I'm having a sort out.'

'Then I won't keep you a moment,' said Anne, 'only I heard you were here again, on the village grapevine, and I thought I'd drop in to say hallo.'

'That was kind,' said Zoe. 'Don't worry about interrupting me, I'm glad of an excuse to stop for a while. Do sit down if you can find a space. It's amazing what people accumulate round them, isn't it? I've just been looking at that box of photographs. There's no one I know, of course, but they're interesting all the same. Would you like a cup of tea?'

'I'd love one if you're going to have one now,' replied Anne, perching on the edge of the table.

'I'll just put the kettle on. I bought a cake, too, yesterday, so we can get started on that.'

As they sat with a cup of tea and huge slice of chocolate cake in front of them, Anne looked across at Zoe and said, 'That's a nasty bruise. What have you been doing to yourself?'

Zoe told her about the burglar the night before.

'Will you be all right here on your own?' asked Anne anxiously.

'I think so. He's hardly likely to come back again now he knows there's someone here,' pointed out Zoe. 'At least, that's what I keep telling myself. Anyway I've got Barney and if he's loose an intruder is less likely to risk coming near, don't you think?'

The two girls had immediately felt a mutual attraction and as they sat and chatted they might have been old friends. Their conversation flowed easily and Zoe told Anne how she had come to inherit the cottage.

'My father left us when I was quite young and then was killed in a car crash soon after. I don't remember him and I never knew any of his family. Then out of the blue I got a letter from this solicitor, telling me my great-aunt Jessie had left me everything, cottage, contents and a little money. I was amazed. I made them check that they'd got the right Zoe Carson; but they had and here I am. Apparently Aunt Jessie had said I deserved something from her because I'd had a difficult start in life due to her nephew.'

'That's fascinating,' said Anne, 'and don't you — ' but she was interrupted by Barney starting to bark. Looking sharply out of the window, Zoe saw Mrs. Penrose sailing up the garden path. Zoe sighed and went to open the front door. Mrs. Penrose surged in preceded by a torrent of words.

'My dear girl, how busy you've been, you look exhausted! What on earth have you done to your cheek? It's a nasty bruise.' She paused long enough for Zoe to explain briefly about the intruder. Mrs. Penrose listened in horror and cried out, 'You really must not think of staying in this house alone another night. You must come to stay with us, James would be delighted. Stay with us until you've sold this horrid place; I shan't know a moment's peace thinking of you here alone with strange men marauding on the cliffs.'

Zoe laughed. 'That really is most kind of you, but I'm not alone, I have Barney for company and now he knows the house is occupied the thief is hardly likely to come back. I expect he thought it was an empty holiday cottage.' Mrs. Penrose was not convinced and tried to insist that Zoe moved across to Shearwater House, but Zoe stood her ground and in the end the old lady admitted defeat and turned her attention to Anne.

'Anne, my dear. I didn't know you were here. I've come to carry Zoe off to tea, but I see you're already having some.'

'Will you have a cup?' asked Zoe hastily, 'I'll just fetch one and put the kettle on for a fresh pot of tea.'

'No, thank you,' said Mrs. Penrose. 'If I can't prevail upon you to come over to us now, I must get back. James'll be in directly. I do hope you'll favour us with your company for tea one day soon.' Mrs. Penrose spoke a little petulantly as she addressed Zoe, and having remained adamant on moving out of the cottage, Zoe felt it would be churlish to refuse the invitation to tea and so she smiled and said, 'That would be lovely. Perhaps I could come tomorrow or the next day.'

'Tomorrow would be convenient,' replied Mrs. Penrose. 'You must come, too,' she added turning to Anne. 'If we're to hold the fête at Shearwater House we must get organised.' Anne agreed and said she would be delighted to join the Penroses for tea the next day.

'Well,' said Mrs. Penrose, apparently satisfied at last, 'I really must go,' and she rose from her chair. Moments later Zoe and Anne were laughing with guilty relief as the redoubtable old lady disappeared up the track towards the road.

'I must go, too,' said Anne. 'David'll wonder where I am.'

'Oh, I meant to say, I've a suitcase of Aunt Jessie's clothes if they're any good to you. Mrs. Penrose suggested you might know somewhere they would be useful.'

'Indeed I do,' said Anne with

enthusiasm, 'the charity shop I help with in Truro.'

'Fine,' said Zoe. 'Would you like them now?'

'I won't take them today if you don't mind,' replied Anne. 'I walked up. Perhaps you could bring them over to Shearwater House tomorrow when I've got the car.'

'Let me run you home in my car now,' said Zoe impulsively.

'Would you? That would be marvellous.'

With the suitcase and Barney in the back, Zoe and Anne drove down to Port Marsden. Drawing up at the vicarage gate they met David Campion arriving home, too, and so Zoe had a chance to meet him again. He was as charming as she had remembered and it was more than half an hour later that she bumped along the track to the cottage. As she saw it she felt a sudden wave of affection for the place so comfortably solid and unperturbed by the years which had passed it by. Pulling up at the garden wall she found the red MGB tucked away round the side of the house and realised Greg had come while she was out. She went to the car, but Greg was nowhere to be seen; passing on into the garden she found him standing by the back door which stood wide open.

'Greg!' she cried in surprise, 'How did you get in?'

'The back door was unlocked so I guessed you hadn't gone far. I hope you didn't mind.'

'No. I should have locked it I suppose. I didn't realise it was open.'

'Well, I must say I was a bit surprised,' admitted Greg, 'after last night I mean. How are you anyway? You look a bit bruised.' He touched her face lightly with his fingers. 'I let the police know first thing this morning.'

'Yes, thank you, a policeman came this morning. He suggested that I change the locks in case there are keys that I don't know about.'

'Good idea,' agreed Greg. 'There's a man in the village who'll do that for you. I know him well, I'll get him to come up tomorrow.'

Zoe smiled gratefully at him. 'Thanks,' she said.

'You had another visitor this afternoon, actually,' went on Greg, 'soon after I arrived.'

'I did?' said Zoe surprised. 'Who was it?'

Greg shrugged. 'Don't know,' he said, 'he didn't stop to say. He was getting out of a green Mini-van, but when he saw me he leapt back into the van and drove off like a madman.'

'Well, I haven't a clue who it was,' said Zoe.

'I thought it might be your friend from London,' said Greg casually.

'Well, it wasn't,' said Zoe sharply. 'He doesn't go around in a Mini-van.'

'No, of course not,' soothed Greg and added with the suspicion of a twinkle in his voice, 'Rolls-Royce, I expect.' Then before Zoe could reply he said, 'I've brought a bottle of wine, let's see if there's a corkscrew in the house.'

Zoe responded to the twinkle, well aware that she rose far too easily to any reference to Robert and said, 'Kitchen drawer, I noticed one yesterday.' And following him back inside she said, 'Is that all you came for?'

'I came to see how you were,' said Greg in a pained voice. 'I've been in Truro today and this is the first chance I've had to make sure you were all right.'

They carried their wine into the early evening garden and sat on a wooden bench leaning against the sun-baked wall of the cottage.

'Actually I came for two other reasons as well. The first is Queen Anne. I've had a word with my father and he's very interested. He's told me a couple of things to look for and he says if you'd like him to come and take a look at her and the one or two other pieces I think are good, he'll be delighted.'

'How kind,' smiled Zoe. 'I'd love him to look if you really think he wouldn't mind.'

'I know he'd like nothing more,' said Greg. 'Anything old fascinates him. He'd be very interested in the cottage itself. After all, that must be nearly three hundred years, or part of it is anyway.'

Zoe was surprised. 'Is it that old?'

'I don't know for sure,' admitted Greg, 'but I should think it dates back to the early eighteenth century anyway. Shearwater House certainly does and this was probably built about the same time.'

Zoe then told him about her promised visit to Shearwater House.

'I don't really want to go,' she said, 'but Mrs. Penrose was so pressing I couldn't get out of it.'

Greg sympathised, for he knew Mrs. Penrose of old. He topped up their glasses before he said casually, 'That's the other reason I've come actually, to bring you another invitation.'

'An invitation? Who from? Where to?'

'From my father, to lunch on Sunday. Would you like to go? I'd pick you up in the morning and bring you back later on. You could tell him about Queen Anne yourself then.'

Zoe was touched and said, 'That sounds lovely, Greg. I'd really like that. How kind of your father.'

Gregory looked pleased.

'Good that's settled then. Let's go and look at Queen Anne so that we can answer my father's queries. I've brought a big torch this time so we can really see.'

Together they went down the cellar steps, their way lit by the beam of Greg's torch. Pausing at the bottom of the steps he swung the flashlight round and Zoe, noticing something in the shaft of light, cried, 'Look Greg, there's a light in the middle of the ceiling. Where's the switch?' Gregory searched the walls with the beam and found the switch next to some pipes which ran along the wall at the bottom of the steps. He flicked it down and the centre light came on.

Turning off the torch and putting it

on the stone stairs, Greg said, 'That's much better. Now let's see about Queen Anne. I want to try and pull her clear of the wall. Do you think you could go the other end? She'll be terribly heavy, I'm afraid.' Zoe went to the far end of the huge bookcase and was about to brace herself against it when she saw something they might have missed if they had still been working by torchlight. There, in the thick layer of dust which covered the whole of Queen Anne, was the print of a man's hand, just where she was about to place her own.

'Greg,' she called, 'come and look at this.'

'What is it?' Greg left his end and came to look.

'Someone's been here, quite recently, too. Look at this, it must have been made by a man, it's a very large print.'

Gregory stared at the tell-tale mark.

'Perhaps it's mine,' he said slowly. 'Perhaps I put my hand there when we came down before.'

Zoe considered this and then said, 'I don't think so. We only looked by torchlight and I don't think either of us put our hands round the back here. You tried to open the top drawer, that's all.'

Greg shrugged. 'Well maybe it's been here for some time. Come on, let's try and move her away from the wall.' He went back to the other end and strained at it, managing to move it a few inches clear of the stone wall. Zoe placing her hands almost on top of the handprint in the dust, heaved as well, but could not move her end an inch.

'I can't shift it at all,' she gasped.

'I've moved it a bit. Come up my end and we'll try together.' Zoe joined Greg and shoulder to shoulder they pushed and pulled, straining and heaving until they had managed to ease one end of the great bookcase a foot or more from the wall.

'Now I want to look at the back,' said Greg and then stopped in surprise as he peered round behind the massive piece of furniture.

'Zoe,' he said, 'there's a door behind here; a great heavy door with bolts drawn across.'

'Let me see!' cried Zoe excitedly, and she edged in beside Greg.

'Perhaps it's another cellar,' she said. 'Let's see if it'll open.'

Greg reached in to pull back the bolts but they were stiff and he squeezed out again and said, 'We'll have to move Queen Anne further out.' Working from the other end of the bookcase this time, they manhandled it further away from the wall so that they could get to the hidden door more easily. Greg drew back the bolts which squeaked in protest as he did so. Then he turned the handle and the door swung open on well-oiled hinges. He was surprised how quietly, but only said to Zoe, 'Get the torch, we'll explore.'

Zoe darted back and picked up the torch. She waited with mounting excitement as Greg pushed the door wide open and shone the torch inside. As he did so a strange smell wafted out and made Zoe wrinkle her nose, the thick, sweet unpleasant smell of foetid air, stale and foul. She held back a little, letting Greg go first, but hurriedly stepped forward again when she heard Greg gasp, forcing her way past his restraining hand to see for herself. In the light of the wavering torch she saw, and clutching at Greg, buried her face in his shoulder to blot out the sight. Lying in a crumpled heap on the floor was a man, his shirt bloodstained and his face turned from them deathly pale. Gregory snapped the torch off the man's body and flashing it quickly round the tiny room beyond the door saw that it was sparsely furnished with table, chair and camp bed. On the table stood a camping gas light, unlit. He slipped his arms round Zoe who was shivering against him and held her close, trying to conceal his own shock as he supported her.

'Come on, Zoe,' he said gently but firmly, 'we must get help.'

6

Zoe allowed Gregory to lead her back through the cellar and up the stairs to the kitchen. There he sat her on a chair and said, 'I must go down again to see if he's alive.' He paused and said hesitantly, 'I — I think he's not, but we must be sure.' Zoe nodded and sat with her face in her hands trying to blot out the picture of the crumpled, blood-stained body which seemed imprinted on her mind. Gregory turned resolutely back to the cellar; moments later he returned.

'No doubt about it, I'm afraid,' he said. 'I'll have to go for the police.'

'You're not leaving me here,' cried Zoe in alarm. 'I'm not staying here on my own with . . . ' she shuddered, 'with him, down there.'

'No, of course not,' said Greg reassuringly. 'We'll both go. I should leave Barney in your car, there's going to be quite a lot happening here soon, I'm afraid.' Gregory locked the cellar door and took the key with him, then together they checked that both the outside doors were locked before Gregory drove them down to the village to find P.C. Dewar.

The rest of the evening passed in a whirl as police cars and an ambulance roared up to the cottage. A police doctor and some C.I.D. men came from Truro and a police photographer moved into the cellar to take photographs of everything before it was touched.

Zoe sat with Greg in the sitting room waiting to know more. A plainclothes inspector named Ferris had asked them a few questions and then vanished down the cellar steps, saying he would want to speak to them again later. Zoe had stopped shaking by now, but felt very tired. She was glad Greg was with her, that she did not have to sit alone, an island of fear in the sea of police activity. She still had no brandy in the house, but Gregory collected the wine they had been drinking earlier and they finished the bottle sitting waiting for Inspector Ferris to return.

At last they heard people coming round the house and saw, through the window, two men carrying a stretcher to the ambulance. Zoe shuddered again as she saw the motionless form lying on the stretcher covered with a white sheet. Gret put a comforting arm round her and she rested against him, glad of his strength.

'It's all right now,' he said, 'they've taken him away.'

The living room door opened and the inspector came in. He was a very tall man and had to duck his head to come through the door. He smiled wearily at Zoe and Greg.

'Thank you for waiting,' he said. 'I'd just like to ask a few more questions, if I may.'

'Of course,' said Zoe, a little more composed now she had heard the ambulance drive off with its dreadful load. 'Do sit down.' The inspector folded himself down into an arm chair and drew out a notebook. Greg perched on the arm of Zoe's chair and waited. The inspector glanced over a page in his book and then looked up.

'Now,' he said, 'perhaps you could explain in a little more detail the circumstances surrounding you finding the body.' So Zoe explained about the cottage, and Inspector Ferris said, 'Just a minute now, did anyone know you'd inherited this place?'

'Several people,' said Zoe. 'I'd been down for a weekend before.'

'Let's face it, Inspector,' put in Greg, 'the whole of Port Marsden knew, it's only a village.'

The inspector smiled at this and said, 'Very probably, sir.' He turned back to Zoe. 'Did anyone know you were coming this time, when you arrived on,' he checked his notes, 'on Sunday?'

'No, it was rather a sudden decision.'

'I see.'

'Why do you want to know?' asked Gregory. 'How long had the man been dead?'

'Not all that long,' replied the inspector, 'about twenty-four hours.'

Zoe turned to Gregory aghast. 'Greg! We heard him. When we were in the cellar yesterday we heard that scratching sound.'

'What? When?'

'You know when we first found Queen Anne; you said it might be rats.' Gregory shrugged. 'It might have been, I suppose,' he said, 'but what I don't understand is how he got there in the first place.' He looked enquiringly at Inspector Ferris who replied, 'He was hiding, or rather being hidden.'

Zoe stared. 'Hidden? Why? Who was he?'

'His name,' said the inspector, 'was William Henry Jarvis. He escaped from Dartmoor prison on Sunday. He certainly had outside help for that, so I imagine he was hidden here until he could be got abroad. He was on a sort of escape route.'

'You mean he's been there ever since I got here?'

'Yes,' said the inspector. 'He was wounded in the escape, he had cuts and bruises on his face and one deep gash on his arm. In the hurry to get him hidden his helper did little more than tie a rough bandage round his arm. Obviously whoever helped him meant to come back later on, next day perhaps.'

'Only I was here,' said Zoe slowly, 'and they couldn't get to him.' She paled further as the full implication hit her.

'Exactly,' said Inspector Ferris.

'But how did he die? I mean he didn't starve in that time, did he?'

'We shan't know for sure until after the postmortem, but it was probably as the result of a blow to his head, perhaps during the escape. There's some buising on the side of his face just above the eye. Now, I understand from Constable Dewar that you had an intruder here last night, Miss Carson.'

'Yes,' replied Zoe shakily. 'Of course, you mean he was trying to get into the cellar.'

'It is possible, particularly as you thought nothing had been taken.'

'But he didn't get in because we disturbed him.'

'That, too, is possible,' agreed the inspector, 'but if he had only got as far as the porch, why didn't he run off as you drove up? You did arrive in a car, I take it?'

Zoe nodded. 'Mr. Enodoc brought me home.' She glanced up at Gregory.

'And your car is the sports car outside, sir?' enquired the inspector.

'Yes, that's mine.'

'Not a quiet car, I daresay, sir?'

Greg grinned. 'Not particularly.'

'Then I think it's fair to assume that the man was already in the house and was letting himself out through the front door when he heard the car.'

'But how did he get in?' cried Zoe. 'We checked everywhere and there was no sign of a forced entry. Constable Dewar looked again this morning.'

'Perhaps he had a key, after all he must have got Jarvis down there in the first place.'

'But not that way,' said Gregory suddenly, 'not into the secret room the way we went in.'

Inspector Ferris looked up sharply.

'Oh,' he said, 'what makes you say that?'

'Because when we moved Queen Anne away from the wall,' explained Gregory, 'it took two of us all our strength to shift her. If people had moved her once already to get the man in it would have taken two, and they would have known that. One could never have reached him, and only one tried.'

'That's a very interesting point, sir,' said Inspector Ferris, 'very interesting. You mean they knew there was an entrance, but not that that enormous bookcase was in the way?'

'Anyway,' put in Zoe, 'it was covered

with dust, it couldn't have been moved for ages. Except . . . '

'Except what?' said the inspector.

'Except,' said Zoe thoughtfully, 'that there was a handprint in the dust on the side where someone had, perhaps, tried to pull or push the bookcase away from the hidden door.'

The inspector was on his feet immediately, 'Come and show me,' he said and followed by a reluctant Zoe and an intrigued Gregory, he led the way back to the cellar. Other police were still busy, but their energies were concentrated on the secret room beyond the door. No time had yet been given to the main cellar and Queen Anne stood exactly where Gregory and Zoe had left her, sticking out into the middle of the room. Zoe paused on the steps, loathe to return to the cellar; Greg noticing her apprehension, gave her hand a reassuring squeeze and led the way. Zoe took a deep breath and stepped down.

'My end,' she said and crossed to the

end of the bookcase which she had tried to move. She peered again at the place she had seen the print in the dust, but the handprint had gone, smudged to an indistinct smear where she had put her own hands in her efforts to move the great bookcase.

'It was here,' she said pointing, 'but I must have rubbed it away when we were trying to move this thing.'

'Pity,' said the inspector. 'Never mind, can't be helped. But what is interesting is how they got into the inner cellar if not through here.'

He edged between Queen Anne and the wall and went through into the secret room.

'I'm not going back in there,' said Zoe firmly. 'I'm never going through that door again.'

'All right,' said Greg, 'but I want to have another look. You wait here, I'll be out again in a minute.' He followed the inspector through the door. It took Zoe two seconds to decide that she would rather brave the inner cellar in company than stand alone in the outer and taking a deep breath she, too, went through the hidden door.

The little room was brightly lit now, with portable spotlights trailing wires out up to the kitchen. She saw the walls were boarded over with vertical planks of wood, like floorboards set on end, though the floor itself was stone with a light covering of sand. Zoe saw the little camping light on the table.

'Why didn't he have the light on?' she said with a cry in her voice. 'Why did he die in the dark?'

'Gas ran out,' said the inspector, his voice matter-of-fact. He turned back to his sergeant and continued to explain matters to him.

'There must be another entrance to this room,' he said. 'I'm almost certain they didn't bring him in this way. You find that, and discover why they couldn't take him out by the same route and we'll be getting somewhere.' The sergeant nodded and turned away to begin a minute search, Inspector

Ferris gave his attention to Zoe and Gregory once again.

'I think it would be better if you took Miss Carson back upstairs. It can only be distressing for her to be in here and we don't want anything else touched until the fingerprint people have finished.'

'Come on, Zoe,' said Greg. 'Let's get out of the way. The inspector will tell us if they find anything else.' He took her arm and led her, unprotesting, back up to the living room. The dusk had deepened outside and darkness crept across the cliff enclosing the little cottage. Greg put on the lights and settled Zoe into a chair by the window before going back into the kitchen to make them some coffee.

'Now then,' he said as he handed her a mug, 'let's get this straight: you are not, repeat not, staying here alone tonight.' Zoe agreed but was at a loss to know where else to go.

'I can't run away from the place,' she said, 'and I've nowhere to go.'

Greg said innocently, 'You could always go to Shearwater House.' His intention to make Zoe smile succeeded, she even laughed as she said vehemently, 'No, thank you!'

'Seriously though, I think you ought to be somewhere else tonight. How about the vicarage? I'd offer you a sofa at my place, but this is a small village and it wouldn't be wise.'

Zoe considered the vicarage and loathe to spend the night alone in the cottage, she allowed herself to be persuaded. Gregory told the police where she was going and then drove her and Barney into Port Marsden and up to the vicarage door.

Anne Campion answered the bell and though surprised to see them standing on her doorstep at almost eleven o'clock at night, one look at Zoe's pale, strained face told her something was wrong and she invited them inside, calling over her shoulder to her husband to come at once. David Campion appeared from his study and

102

led them all into the sitting room.

'Now then,' he said, 'tell us what's happened.' He and Anne listened in silence as Zoe and Gregory between them told of the evening's events. When they had finished David Campion said, 'That's incredible; it all sounds very strange, as if what's happened tonight is only the tip of the iceberg.'

'That's what I feel,' said Gregory at once. 'There's much more to this than meets the eye. In the first place how did this man, Jarvis, or whatever his name is, how did he get into the hiding place?'

'We can't go into all that now,' put in Anne firmly. 'Zoe looks all in and I'm going to make up the spare bed. You were quite right to bring her here, Greg.' She turned to Zoe. 'You can't possibly go back to that cottage for a day or two. You must stay here as long as you like.'

'Thank you,' said Zoe gratefully, and wishing the vicar and Gregory good-night, she followed Anne upstairs, leaving the men to their discussion.

When she woke in the morning, Zoe lay for one glorious moment without recalling the horror of the previous night; then as she consciously recognised her surroundings as the vicarage spare bedroom, she sat up with a jerk and it all came flooding back to her, and the same ominous foreboding settled on her spirit. This was dispelled somewhat when she went down to breakfast in the homely vicarage kitchen. Anne was cheerful and the morning sunny, and gradually the horror receded, kept at bay by normality.

Zoe spent the rest of the week at the vicarage and grew to like both the Campions immensely. She was at ease in their company and David made a splendid buffer to shelter her from the influx of reporters and photographers. He dealt with them firmly, keeping them at bay, and allowed only Gregory, James and Mrs. Penrose in to see her. Zoe wished he had kept Mrs. Penrose at bay, too, but knew it was impossible and prepared herself for the inevitable flood of questions.

'My dear, how terrifying to have been alone in the cottage with that man. Had you heard anything? Sounds in the night? Cries or knockings?'

Zoe assured her she had not.

'I should have been so frightened,' said Mrs. Penrose. 'A criminal in the cellar! You could have been murdered in your bed.'

Zoe smiled. 'Hardly that, Mrs. Penrose. He was trapped in there. No one could move that bookcase alone.'

'If he could get in, he could get out,' declared Mrs. Penrose, stubbornly.

'Not through the cottage,' said Zoe.

'How did he get in then?' demanded Mrs. Penrose. 'Have the police discovered that?'

'There's another entrance,' explained Zoe. 'The inspector came to see me again and told me they'd found a sort of swing door in the wooden panelling of the inner cellar and beyond it was a tunnel.'

'A tunnel!' said Mrs. Penrose sharply. 'Where does it lead to?'

'To the cliff, but . . . ' began Zoe.

'Then why couldn't the man get out that way instead of dying in your cellar?'

'The main tunnel leads towards the sea,' said Zoe, 'but there's been a roof fall and it's blocked.'

'If it's blocked,' said Mrs. Penrose persistently, 'how did he get in?'

'The police think that he was already in the secret room before the rockfall. If you remember that part of the cliff collapsed on Sunday night. They think the passage became blocked then. That's why no help could reach the man that way and they tried to get in through the cottage.'

'Mmm,' said Mrs. Penrose suddenly losing interest, 'sounds far-fetched to me.' And to Zoe's relief she began to discuss the forthcoming fête.

David arranged to have the locks changed on the cottage doors and presenting Zoe with a new set of keys, said, 'We want to be sure no one but you can get in without your permission,' and Zoe shuddered to think that until then someone else had had access to her house and possibly used it in her absence for his own purposes. She gave a spare key to Gregory so that he could show prospective buyers around, but felt more comfortable in the knowledge that the door was locked and no one else could enter the cottage whilst she was staying at the vicarage.

Both Anne and David accompanied her to the brief inquest on William Jarvis where a verdict of accidental death was returned. Zoe was very grateful for their support; for although she had little to contribute beyond the fact that he was found in her house, which Gregory corroborated, it was not a very pleasant experience and she was glad when it was over.

7

Gregory collected Zoe from the vicarage on Sunday, after morning service and drove her to his father's home about ten miles away. By tacit consent they did not discuss Jarvis, or the secret room, and as they sped along the country lanes with the roof off the car and the summer sun beating down on their heads, Zoe felt the last vestiges of her depression blow away into the scent of summer. She had telephoned the office once the news of the discovery of Jarvis's body had hit the headlines, feeling that the sound of Robert's voice would make her feel better, but he had been out and though she had left the vicarage phone number, he had not returned her call.

He's probably still very busy tying up the loose ends on the American deal, she thought firmly, but she wished he would ring and each shrill of the vicarage telephone made her heart stand still for a moment until she was sure that the call was not for her.

Gregory, perhaps sensing her mood, chatted easily and started to tell her about his father.

'My mother died several years ago,' he said, 'but my father still lives in the same house and is looked after by his housekeeper, Mrs. Mitchell. It is she who rules the roost while appearing to defer to him. They get on famously.'

'And your father's retired?' asked Zoe.

'Well, officially, yes,' said Greg, 'but he's not the retiring sort. He's always got some ploy on hand to keep him busy; he loves going to antique sales to see what he can find. Gets a great kick if he thinks he's outwitted a dealer.'

'Does he know a lot about antiques?'

'Quite a bit,' said Greg, 'furniture particularly. In fact there are several dealers who watch him at sales to see which pieces take his fancy. That pleases him, too, I think.'

'Were you brought up where your father lives now?'

'Charfield Manor? Yes, it's been in the family for more than a hundred years.'

Zoe raised her eyebrows when she heard the name of the Enodocs' home.

'A manor house? I didn't realise I was hobnobbing with the local gentry.' Greg laughed and the sound of his laugh, spontaneous, rich and natural, made Zoe laugh, too, and in easy companionship they drove through the village of Charfield and turned in through the open wrought-iron gates of the manor house drive.

The sight of the house itself made Zoe catch her breath and say impulsively, 'Oh, Greg, what a beautiful house!'

Gregory looked pleased and said simply, 'We think so, but I must admit you're seeing it at its best.'

The house was long and low, reclining in its sunlit garden. Its grey stone walls were mellowed by the age-old creeper which covered them and its windows, tall and mullioned, peered out from between the leaves, their casements thrown open to the summer. The drive opened into a turning circle before the heavy front door, strong against the Cornish winter, but open now in welcome. As Greg drew the car to a halt his father appeared round the side of the house and hurried forward to open the car door for Zoe with an old-world courtesy. Zoe, looking up at from the low car seat, was met by Greg's blue eyes set in an older version of his face. She could see at once what Gregory would look like in another thirty years. Even his welcoming smile was the same and Zoe felt she knew him already as she placed her hand in his proffered one and allowed herself to be helped from the car.

'Dad, this is Zoe,' said Gregory, easing his long legs from the car and walking round to join them.

'So I see,' said his father. 'How do you do, Zoe?'

'Very well, thank you,' she replied, returning his smile and noticing as she did so the flicker of appreciation in the older man's eyes as he looked at her. Suddenly flattered, she was glad she had taken care over her appearance today; often whilst on holiday she was content to dress very casually, in sharp contrast with her neat and formal office clothes, but today she had selected a cool, creamy sundress which showed off her smooth skin, tanned golden by the sun, and had left her long dark hair loose, though knotted with a russet scarf for the journey in the open car. This scarf she now removed and her hair gleamed in the sunshine, glossy black with a hint of hidden red. She looked good and sudden recognition of the fact gave her unexpected confidence. She felt she was going to enjoy her day.

'Come through to the terrace,' said Gregory and detaching her neatly from his father, led them through the wide front door into the cool hall beyond.

The house was as lovely inside as it appeared from the out. The hall, lofty and cool held little furniture, but there was a heavy oak chest with gleaming brass handles and a beautiful Indian rug on the polished floor. A faint but distinct smell of lavender pervaded the air and Zoe knew immediately how much loving attention was given to the care of this house. Greg opened one of the doors which led off the hall and took her into a sun-drenched drawing room with French doors thrown open to the garden beyond.

'You bring us some drinks out on to the terrace, Greg, while I make Zoe comfortable,' Mr. Enodoc said.

Greg disappeared back through the hall and Mr. Enodoc led Zoe out on to the terrace. Sheltered on two sides by high stone walls it was a sun-trap and Zoe was soon settled on the comfortable swing seat while Mr. Enodoc flopped into an old-fashioned rocking chair.

'I can see no point in being uncomfortable merely because one is sitting in the garden,' he explained. 'Too many people these days throw a few deck chairs on to their lawns and are surprised when they get stiff from sitting in them.' He went on almost without pause, 'I was sorry to hear of the unpleasant happenings at your cottage; I do hope it won't put you off the place.'

'Well,' said Zoe, not unwilling to discuss the subject now it had been broached, 'I didn't intend to keep it anyway, you know. It's on the market and I shall sell it at the first decent offer I get. I only hope that the finding of the body doesn't frighten away the buyers.'

'It might some, I suppose,' said Mr. Enodoc, considering, 'but on the other hand it might work the other way; you know, fascination of the horrible. People might be attracted out of interest and then find they liked the place.'

Zoe shuddered, 'They'd be a bit odd, I think.'

'Who would?' enquired Greg appearing through the drawing room doors carrying a tray of drinks. 'I've done a Pimms,' he said, setting the tray down. 'Something long and cool for such a hot day.' Zoe accepted the tall glass he offered and sipped the drink. It was delicious.

'Have you had anyone interested in Zoe's cottage yet?' Greg's father asked.

'Several people have had details and I've taken one couple round but there's been nothing more than that.'

'Greg said you might come and have a look at the furniture for me,' said Zoe, turning to Mr. Enodoc. 'He says you'll know what I should try to sell separately and what I can let go with the cottage.'

'Certainly, my dear. I should be delighted. I'm particularly interested in the secretaire bookcase Greg's described to me. If it's what I think it is and you are putting it on the market I shall very likely make an offer for it myself.'

The conversation turned to antiques

in general and Zoe found Mr. Enodoc's knowledge fascinating. He was certainly knowledgeable about furniture in general, but was also able to relate little snippets of history connected with individual pieces he owned or had come across.

'After lunch,' he said, 'I shall show you my latest acquisition.'

'What have you been buying now, Dad?' asked Greg with a grin.

'A library.' Mr. Enodoc's voice was solemn but his eyes sparkled with delight.

'A library!' Zoe was incredulous.

'Yes,' replied Mr. Enodoc, 'old General Haworth over at Rusham Grange died recently and the whole place came under the hammer. Damned shame really, beautiful old house.'

'Yes,' said Greg, 'I knew the house was up for sale, a big firm in Plymouth has got it.'

'That's right,' agreed his father. 'Well, the sale of the contents was last week and I bought his library. It all needs cataloguing of course, but I believe there are several good first editions and lots of other interesting things as well. That'll be my winter job this year and I'm really looking forward to it.'

After an excellent lunch provided by Mrs. Mitchell, Mr. Enodoc showed Zoe round the house, enlivening the tour with stories of previous owners, many of whom stared down at them from huge gloomy frames in a room Mr. Enodoc described as the 'Rogues Gallery'. Then at last he took her into the library and showed her a stack of wooden crates standing in the corner.

'There,' he said proudly, waving a hand towards them, 'those are what I bought at Rusham Grange.' Zoe looked round the room which was already lined from ceiling to floor with books, many of them leather bound, their spines lettered in gold. There was a comfortable leathery smell mingled with wood smoke and pipe tobacco, and Zoe knew that this was Mr. Enodoc's own room, where he sat or worked when he was alone.

'This is a lovely room,' she said, and Mr. Enodoc smiled, 'I think so, too,' he said. 'I always work here if I can,' and Zoe could imagine him there, a log fire in the grate and the heavy red velvet curtains drawn against the night, happily poring over his books or settled in his huge leather armchair reading the paper.

'But if those crates are full of books,' she said, 'where are you going to put them?' Mr. Enodoc grinned and Zoe recognised Greg once again in his smile.

'Don't worry,' he said, 'I'll find space. There may be duplicates or better editions than some of mine; I'll sort them all out. I may even get someone to help me.' He looked speculatively at Zoe. 'Would you like the job?'

'Me!' exclaimed Zoe in surprise. 'But I don't know anything about cataloguing libraries.'

'Maybe not,' said Mr. Enodoc, 'but I do, and with common sense and an organising mind which you must have to hold down your present job, you'd soon learn.' Zoe laughed a little uncertainly and then said, 'I'm afraid I can't be of help to you there, I'm off back to London at the end of the week. I'm only on holiday, you know.'

'Of course you are,' said Mr. Enodoc and before he could say more, Greg appeared at the library door.

'There you are,' he said, 'I might have known. Anyway Dad, you've monopolised Zoe long enough, it's my turn now. Do you feel like a walk, Zoe?'

'Good idea,' said Mr. Enodoc. 'You can work up an appetite for tea.'

Zoe and Greg crossed the lawn to the orchard beyond and then struck out across the fields towards a wooded hill.

'There's a marvellous view from the top,' said Greg. 'Although we're several miles inland here you can see the sea on a clear day like today.'

It was very hot and by the time they had scrambled to the top of the hill they were both panting and red in the face. Zoe flung herself down on the springy grass and buried her face in its coolness. Greg flopped down beside her and for a moment neither of them spoke. Glancing up, Zoe found Greg watching her intently and turned away, confused, the colour flooding to her face.

'I'm glad you get on so well with my father,' said Greg easily, apparently unaware of her discomposure. 'He loves to have visitors, for although he keeps himself so busy I think he gets quite lonely.'

'I think he's charming,' said Zoe, still gazing steadfastly out towards the sea; she turned her head at last and added lightly, 'He's offered me a job.'

'Has he now?' Greg sounded amused, 'I said he was feeling lonely. And have you accepted?'

Zoe laughed. 'No, of course not. I'm back off up to London next weekend.'

'So you are,' said Greg and added, 'so I'd better bring Dad over before then to have a look at Queen Anne and the other things. We'll fix a time with him before we leave.'

They spent the rest of the afternoon rambling in a circuitous route back to Charfield Manor and arrived just as Mrs. Mitchell carried in the tea tray.

'I saw you coming across the field and knew you'd be ready for a cup of tea,' she said.

'Thank you, Mrs. Mitchell, you were quite right,' said Greg.

Mr. Enodoc appeared from the library and said, 'Will you pour, Zoe? I hate to see men wielding a teapot when there's a lady present.' Zoe took her place and picked up the teapot.

After tea Mr. Enodoc asked Zoe to excuse him and Greg for half an hour, as they had some business to discuss.

'The Sunday papers are on the table, my dear, and the sun's still on the terrace if you want to sit outside.'

Zoe picked up the pile of newspapers and carried them out to the swing seat. Adjusting its canopy to shade her eyes, she swung her legs up in front of her and swinging gently, began to scan the papers. One paper was folded inside out and it was not until she had read several articles that she realised she was reading the previous day's *Times*. She was about to lay it aside and turn her attention to the Sunday colour supplement, when a name caught her eye and she jerked the paper sharply back towards her. There was no doubt, and as she re-read the announcement her heart seemed to pause and she was suddenly stone cold; there at the top of the engagement announcements column was Robert's name.

'*Robert Stackton only son of the late Mr. and Mrs. Daniel Stackton to Rosemary Jane Spark, elder daughter of Colonel and Mrs. Andrew Spark.*'

She stared blindly at the print as her heart repeatedly stammered out the words, Robert's going to marry Rosemary, Robert's going to marry Rosemary. When Greg and his father joined her on the terrace sometime later, Zoe had her emotions firmly under control and though pale under her tan she smiled, and though her laughter was brittle, she laughed. Once she caught Greg glancing at her interrogatively, but she ignored the question in his eyes and spoke to his father. The newspaper with its shattering announcement lay buried at the bottom of the pile of Sundays, the offending page returned to the inside.

Before long Greg said that he thought it was time to make a move, and though his father looked disappointed at what he obviously regarded as their early departure, he made no comment and when they had arranged a time for him to come over to Shearwater Cottage to look at the furniture, Greg tucked Zoe back into his car and drove out through the gates back to Port Marsden. They drove in silence for a while and then he said, 'Penny for them, Zoe.'

'Not worth a penny,' returned Zoe lightly.

'Don't want to talk?'

'What about?' Zoe sounded defensive and immediately Greg was soothing.

'Nothing in particular. You're not worried about the cottage are you?'

Zoe shook her head. 'Anyway I'll stay at the vicarage for another couple of days, I expect. Anne and David have invited me to stay all this week too, if I want to.'

'It'd probably be a good idea,' said Greg and the silence slid back round them with only the roar of the engine to break it.

'Would you like to stop for a drink?' asked Greg a little later. 'There's a nice pub in the next village.'

'Do you mind if we don't?' said Zoe. 'I'm a bit tired and I'd like to get an early night.' As she heard her own voice speaking, another part of her was saying, 'Why fool yourself, you won't sleep tonight.'

'Of course, I'll take you straight back then.' And the silence settled round them again until the car wound its way down the steep hill into Port Marsden and drew up outside the vicarage. Then Greg spoke gently.

'Is there anything I can do to help?' The soft concern in his voice was nearly the undoing of Zoe, her rigid control almost at breaking point. She shook her head, though part of her ached to tell him, longed to be sheltered in his arms and comforted, the last vestige of her pride held her aloof and she forced a tight smile to her lips and said, 'It really has been a lovely day, Greg. Thank you for taking me over to meet your father. I must go in now.' She fumbled with the car door handle and he made no move to restrain her, and Zoe was grateful, for if he had she knew she would have clung to him and wept. Instead he reached over and opened the door for her and then getting out himself, walked her up the path to the vicarage front door.

8

Safely in the sanctuary of her room, Zoe relaxed the hold on herself and the tears streamed down her face. She lay on her bed and cried until she was drained and as the grey dawn fingered the night sky she finally drifted into an uneasy sleep, only to awake, heavy-eyed and tired a few hours later. She lay on her back staring up at the ceiling and tried to concentrate her mind on what she should do.

'I'll ring Robert at the office this morning,' she decided and feeling fractionally better for having made some sort of decision, she got up.

David had finished his breakfast and retired to his study by the time Zoe came downstairs, but Anne was still in the kitchen and pouring herself another cup of coffee settled down at the table again as Zoe struggled to force down a piece of toast and drink a cup of coffee.

'Out with it,' Anne said with no preamble, 'you look terrible. What on earth's the matter?' So Zoe told her and as she did so Anne poured her another cup of coffee and Zoe found the telling and the hot coffee both helped.

'It obviously all happened on the trip to America. He didn't take Rosemary because Mr. Paterson would need her, but because he did. No wonder he didn't take me along, too,' Zoe laughed bitterly, 'and that's why he was sort of different when he came back; keeping me at arm's length. Anyway, I thought I'd ring up today and — '

'What for?' interrupted Anne.

Zoe looked surprised. 'What do you mean, what for?'

'I mean,' said Anne, 'why ring up? You know they're engaged, that they're going to be married, what you've got to do is make the break and put it all behind you.'

'Make the break?' Zoe was startled.

'Well, it's up to you, of course,' said

Anne, 'but if it were me, I'd find it very difficult to go on working in the office as if nothing had happened.'

'At least I'd see him every day,' said Zoe.

'You would, and that would be the worst possible thing. Why torture yourself by being so near and yet so far? You might see him every day, but he'll be going home to Rosemary every night.' She spoke with calculated harshness. 'Every morning he'll have come from her. You'll be constantly aware of him and yet living without hope, fuelling your own heartache until you get all hard and bitter.' Zoe stared at her dumbly, and Anne continued more gently, 'It's time to move on, Zoe. Cut loose and start again.'

'I must talk to him,' said Zoe stubbornly. 'I must, that's all.'

'Fine,' said Anne lightly, 'you do that. Tell him you're leaving.' She got up from the table and began to stack the things on to the draining board. 'David's going to a meeting in half an hour, you can use the study phone.'

'But I can't just throw up my job like that,' cried Zoe. 'I can't just walk out on him after so long.'

'Does he know how you feel about him?' asked Anne.

'No, of course not,' replied Zoe. 'Well, I suppose he might. I mean, well, he must have some idea.'

'Then perhaps it would be easier for him, too,' pointed out Anne, 'if you weren't there after he's married.'

'Well, he probably won't be married for a long time yet.'

'So you'll hang around until he is?' Anne spoke with her back to Zoe, her hands in a sink full of bubbles, washing up the breakfast things. Zoe did not answer the question, but gulped down the last of her coffee and said, 'Will you give me a call when David's gone out?' before she retreated once more to her bedroom.

It was almost an hour later when Anne called to Zoe that the study was free. In the meantime Zoe had done some hard thinking and decided what she was going to say to Robert; even so she felt very shaky as she perched on the edge of David's desk and dialled the office number. The switchboard answered and Zoe said, 'Mr. Stackton, please.' There was a sharp click and then Robert's voice, crisp and clear.

'Stackton.'

'Robert, it's me, Zoe.' Although she had been expecting him to answer, Robert's familiar voice made her heart turn over and her voice sound shaky.

'Zoe! How nice to hear you. Sorry I didn't return your call last week, but I had a lot on.'

'Yes, I heard,' said Zoe, 'or rather I saw it in The Times. Congratulations, Robert, I hope you and Rosemary will be very happy.'

'Thanks, I'm sure we will.' Deftly he changed the subject. 'How's the holiday going?'

'It was all right to begin with,' said Zoe, 'but after they found the body . . .'

'Yes, of course,' drawled Robert. 'I'd

forgotten about that for the moment. Dreadful business. I expect you'll be even more keen to sell the cottage now.'

'Well, I don't know,' began Zoe, but Robert interrupted, 'Look, Zoe, it's lovely to talk to you, but I must fly. Rosemary and I are due at a meeting in a moment or two.' She heard a girl laugh in the background and Zoe suddenly realised Rosemary was sitting in on Robert's end of the conversation, and something inside her snapped.

Anger welled up and she said abruptly, 'I haven't rung up for a chat, Robert, but to hand in my notice.'

There was silence on the end of the phone for a moment and then Robert said smoothly, 'Of course, Zoe, if that's what you think is best you're probably right; we'll be sorry to lose you.' He paused again and then added, 'I think you're due another three weeks holiday, aren't you? Why don't you make it the month and then you can take it from now and you needn't work your notice.'

'Certainly,' said Zoe calmly, 'that

would suit me very well. I'll come back in a few days to clear my desk.'

'Fine,' said Robert equally calmly, and Zoe heard a woman's voice in the background again, 'unless you'd like us to send you your things. Rosemary says she'll be happy to pack them up for you.'

'No, thank you,' said Zoe firmly, 'I'd rather come myself.'

'Of course,' said Robert heartily. 'We'll see you in a day or two.'

'Wednesday afternoon.'

'Wednesday afternoon.'

'Goodbye Robert,' and Zoe, gently, replaced the receiver.

For a moment Zoe stared round David's study, a comfortable muddle of books, papers and framed photographs.

'Well, I've done it.' Zoe spoke aloud, and added, 'but I didn't mean to; not today anyway. They couldn't wait to get rid of me.' She went out into the hall to find Anne and tell her what she had done.

'Good for you,' said Anne approvingly. 'Now let's decide what you're going to do next.'

They sat down over yet another cup of coffee and Zoe said, 'I'll probably try and get temporary work until something I really want to do turns up. I'll sign on somewhere while I'm in London on Wednesday.'

'You'll stay in London then?'

Zoe looked surprised at the question. 'Of course. Where else?'

'Here,' said Anne simply.

'Here?'

'Why not? You've somewhere to live here, you like the village, you've already made friends, all you have to do is find a job.'

Zoe laughed for the first time since the day before.

'That's easy, I've already been offered one. Greg's father asked me to help him catalogue his new library.'

'There you are then, that's settled.'

'Oh, Anne, don't be so silly. Nothing's settled.'

'Why not?' asked Anne again. 'Specially if you've got a job as well.'

Zoe stared at her helplessly and then said, 'But the cottage is on the market.'

'Take it off then.'

'And Mr. Enodoc probably wasn't serious in his offer of a job. I expect he was joking; I didn't take him seriously anyway.'

'Ring him up and ask him.'

'But I've never lived out of London.'

'Then it's time you did.' Anne smiled at her and said coaxingly, 'Come on, Zoe, take the plunge. You've got nothing to lose, because if you find you don't like it you can always sell up and go. There's nothing to keep you in London now you know.'

'No, nothing to keep me there now,' sighed Zoe.

'Then go and phone Mr. Enodoc now, and if he wasn't serious it doesn't matter. You've got plenty of time to look round for something else.'

So, Zoe went and telephoned Mr. Enodoc. When he heard what she wanted he was enchanted.

'You're really serious, my dear?' he said. 'Because if you are, I should be delighted; I meant it about needing someone, but I didn't think you were in a position to take on the job; I should be delighted if you could. I think we'd work well together.' Zoe agreed and Mr. Enodoc continued, 'But don't cut short your holiday on my account; we needn't get down to work for a week or two yet. Get yourself comfortably settled in that house of yours, and we'll start work when you're ready.'

Mr. Enodoc's pleasure at Zoe's working with him gave her a certain measure of confidence and buoyed up by it, she walked out into the morning sunshine and crossed the harbour square to Grant, Pollard & Co. The receptionist showed her straight into Gregory's office and closed the door behind her.

Greg's face lit up when he saw who it was and he said, 'Zoe, how nice! Is this just a social call?' If he noticed her drawn face and the dark smudges under her eyes he made no comment, but settled her into a chair and waited.

Zoe smiled back and said, 'No, Greg. It's business.' A flicker of disappointment crossed his face, but he said, 'Good. What sort of business? How can I help you?'

Zoe took a deep breath and said, 'I want the cottage off the market.'

Gregory stared at her. 'Off the market?'

'Yes, I've decided to stay.'

'Stay? Permanently you mean? Or to keep it as a holiday cottage?'

'To stay, for a while anyway.' Her face remained impassive; Greg's creased into a wide smile and he said simply, 'I'm glad.'

Zoe was grateful that he did not ask any questions and apparently accepted what she told him, that she had reconsidered his father's offer and decided to give it a try. The only comment he made was very much to the point and caused her to give great thought to it.

'Will you mind living in the cottage alone after what we discovered there?'

At the time she answered the question simply, 'I don't know.' But as she walked up the hill to the vicarage the question haunted her, Will I mind?

By the time she joined David and Anne for lunch her mind was made up and she knew that the decision, once taken, must be implemented at once.

'I've decided what to do,' she announced at the luncheon table; 'I'm going back to the cottage today.' Anne stared at her in dismay and said, 'There's no need to rush back there, Zoe. You're welcome here as long as you like, isn't she, David?'

David nodded his agreement, but added, 'However, I think Zoe's is the right choice. She can't stay away for ever if she has, indeed, decided to make Shearwater Cottage her home. It may not be easy for a little while, but it's something only she can overcome.'

'Well, at least let me come with you,' said Anne, still very concerned. 'We can

137

go round the house together — every bit of it — so that you can lay any ghosts and be quite comfortable there.'

Zoe smiled at her friend gratefully and said, 'Thank you, Anne, that would be a great help. Greg did offer to come, but I wanted to do it alone and refused his offer, but it would be different if it was you.'

'No commitment.'

Zoe looked surprised. 'Commitment? What sort of commitment?'

Anne let the question ride and said, 'We'll go this afternoon; are you all packed up?' Zoe, who had packed her few belongings on her return from Gregory's office, nodded and said, 'I'm quite ready to go.' And Anne said again, 'That's settled then.'

9

It was an hour or so later that David Campion's battered car toiled up the road out of Port Marsden, taking Zoe and her luggage back to Shearwater Cottage. Anne was driving, concentrating on coaxing the old car up the steep hill and Zoe had a moment to reflect on what she felt about returning to her new home. The afternoon sun beamed down on the world and Zoe's first glimpse of the cottage now was a little different from the first time she had seen it; comfortably settled in its fold in the cliff and drowsily dreaming, it no longer seemed forlorn, but waiting for her. For the first time she really viewed it as her home and despite the all too recent spine-chilling memory of the discovery in the cellar, she felt the warmth of the place and when Anne pulled up outside and Zoe clambered out she knew Shearwater Cottage was as pleased to have her back as she was to return.

Leaving Barney to re-explore and reclaim the garden and surrounding cliff top, Zoe and Anne opened the front door and went inside; Anne keeping up a steady flow of bright chatter as if to ward off evil spirits. But Zoe was assailed by none and happily carried her case up to the large bedroom, flinging wide the window to the sea air and allowing the steady pounding of the waves at the foot of the cliff to soothe away the last cobwebs of fear.

It was Anne who had said, safely ensconced in the vicarage kitchen, that they should go round 'every bit' of the cottage, but it was Zoe who turned with determination towards the cellar door. There should be no no-go areas in her home. Barney rushed happily in through the back door and preceded them into the cool dimness below. Anne shivered, but with her courage still high

Zoe switched on the light at the bottom of the steps and looked round her. Queen Anne still stood clear of the wall and behind her was the open doorway to the underground room. The flashlight Greg had used when they first discovered the room stood forgotten on an old packing-case and catching sight of it, Zoe picked it up and crossed, with determination, to the dark doorway.

'Zoe!' whispered Anne tremulously. 'Zoe! Do we really have to go in there?'

'Come on, Anne,' said Zoe firmly, 'last hurdle on this track,' and with Anne close at her shoulder she stepped into the underground room.

It was almost an anti-climax. Everything had been cleared up and the few sticks of furniture might never have been used. As Zoe shone the torch round she was aware only of the silence and the slightly musty air. When she spoke her voice sounded abnormally loud and she lowered it to a stage whisper.

'There, you see, nothing there to be

afraid of. I'll have this doorway closed off and I never need to think of it again.' Emboldened by the very ordinariness of the little room she saw, Anne edged past Zoe and said, 'I wonder who built this place?'

'Perhaps it was just an extra cellar built at the same time as the cottage.'

'Possibly,' agreed Anne, 'but the wooden panelling must be fairly new. Why was that put there?'

Zoe shrugged and shone the torch along the strange wooden walls, 'To conceal the other entrance, I suppose. What are you doing?' Anne had begun tapping the wall opposite the doorway.

'Trying to find the hollow panel. You said there was a sort of swing door and I wondered where it was, that's all.'

'Probably on that wall,' agreed Zoe shifting the torch to her left hand and starting to tap as well. It did not take long to discover where the entrance was, there was a completely different tone when Anne rapped with her knuckles on one particular panel.

'How do you think it opens?' she asked excitedly.

'I don't know, let's try.' Together they pushed and pressed and knocked and tapped, exploring the edges of the panel with their fingers, feeling for a handle or any sort of switch. But they were hampered by the darkness; the room was only dimly lit by the light in the outside cellar and the torch could only pinpoint a small area at a time. At last Zoe sighed and leaned wearily against the wall. 'Stupid door,' she said and thumped her fist against the next panel. There was a soft click and the door section swung away from them leaving a crack of complete darkness in the wall. Both girls stepped back in alarm.

'How did I do that?' cried Zoe in amazement. By the light of the torch they examined the panel where Zoe had banged her hand and saw that there was a brown knot in the wood.

'That must be the catch there,' said Anne, 'when you press that knot you must release the door.'

While they were examining the hidden switch Barney snuffled round their feet and having exhausted the interesting smells in the cellars, slipped between Zoe's legs and disappeared into the darkness beyond the hidden door.

'Barney!' cried Zoe, pushing the door wider and shining the torch after him, 'Barney! Come back!' But hot on the trail of an intriguing smell, Barney ignored her calls and vanished into the underground passageway.

'Barney! Come back, you'll get lost, you silly dog! Barney!' The torchlight revealed a narrow rocky passage twisting away from the cellar room, but there was no sign of Barney.

'I'd better go and fetch him,' said Zoe, sounding braver than she felt. She had been determined to come to grips with the secrets of her cottage, but she was not keen on venturing into the underground passage which twisted away from it beneath the cliffs.

'Don't go,' cried Anne in alarm.

'Don't go in there, call him again. He'll come back.'

Zoe called again, her voice echoing strangely in the rocky passage, but Barney did not appear.

'It's a dead end,' she said, 'the police said so; the passage is blocked by a rockfall. He can't go far.'

But Barney did not return and after waiting and calling for several minutes, Zoe said, 'I really must go and find him. Will you be all right here?'

'No,' said Anne very definitely. 'There is absolutely no way I am going to stand alone here in a dark room where a man died, waiting for you to come back. If we must go we stick together.'

Glad that she did not have to search for Barney alone, Zoe said, 'Well, if you're sure, hang on to me.' She held the torch high in front of her and with Anne holding tightly to the back of her shirt, stepped right through the doorway into the tunnel beyond.

'Zoe!' hissed Anne, and Zoe jerked to

a halt. 'What if this door closes behind us? We might never get out.'

'You're right,' said Zoe. 'Let's wedge it open with something.' She shone the torch back into the little room and when its beam picked out the old wooden chair she said, 'That'll do.' Quickly she placed the chair in the doorway so that it was impossible for the secret panel to swing closed and then with one final call to Barney, they set off along the underground passage.

The pathway was narrow and twisting, sloping gently downwards at first and then going more steeply so that it was almost a rocky staircase. There was no sign of Barney and he did not come in answer to their calls; so they pressed on slowly and found the passage flattened out and widened into a cavern. The beam of the torch, now yellowing a little as its batteries weakened, was unable to pick out the end of the cave from where they stood and so hand in hand, Zoe and Anne advanced slowly across it until they reached the point where it narrowed again. They followed the new passage until it ended suddenly in a pile of rocks, tumbled into an enormous heap, blocking the passage from ceiling to floor.

'Well, here's the rockfall,' said Zoe peering at it through the semi-dark. 'But where has Barney gone?' She shone the torch up the slide of rocks until it met with the rocky ceiling above. There was no way past the fall, even for a small inquisitive dog like Barney.

'He must have turned back,' said Anne.

'But we'd have seen him; he'd have seen us even if we'd missed him.' Zoe felt the fear creeping through her. She tried to keep her voice steady, but it shook a little as she said, 'Perhaps there are other passages off the main one.'

'Well, we're not exploring them,' said Anne firmly. 'We've been down here quite long enough. Barney'll find his own way out; dogs have an uncanny sense of direction. He's probably back in the cellar even now wondering where we are. Come on, Zoe, we must go back.'

It was Anne who took command now and taking the torch from Zoe's unresisting grasp, Anne took her by the arm and led her back along the rocky corridor, picking out their way by the increasingly feeble light of the torch. Suddenly she stopped so abruptly that Zoe stumbled into her.

'What's the matter?' Zoe said sharply.

'Which way?' whispered Anne.

'Just follow the passage we came along,' said Zoe a little irritably.

'But which is it?'

'What do you mean?'

'There's a fork.'

'A fork?' Zoe squeezed up beside Anne and stared at the passageways. 'We can't have come this way, we didn't see a fork as we came.'

'No, because we came down one side of it and in the darkness never saw the other passage opening behind us. We were only looking ahead. We don't know which way to go. We're lost.' Anne sounded panicky.

'Don't be silly,' said Zoe sharply, 'of course we're not lost.'

'Which way then?'

'Right,' said Zoe. 'We'll take the right fork. Come on, I'll lead the way.' She set off up the right hand fork. The passage turned sharply and then plunged downhill again only to narrow until it was impassable.

'This isn't right,' said Zoe. 'We certainly didn't come through this narrow place. Let's go back and take the other fork.' Slowly they retraced their steps, gripping hands and following the increasingly dim beam of the flashlight. Suddenly they found themselves at the rockfall again.

'We've missed it,' exclaimed Zoe. 'Even though we were looking for it we missed that fork; no wonder we didn't notice it the first time.'

'Never mind that,' snapped Anne, 'we've got to find it this time or we shan't be able to see at all. We'll have no light.' There was barely suppressed panic in her voice and Zoe spoke with a calm she was far from feeling, 'Don't worry, we'll see it all right going this way.'

She was right, before long the faint beam of the torch showed them the fork and this time they took the left hand fork and found themselves back in the underground cavern. They could not see the far side of it, but were aware that they were in a space much wider than the enclosed passage they had been following.

'We'll follow the wall round until we find the opening,' said Zoe, 'rather than cross the middle of the cave and perhaps lose our bearings.'

'I've lost mine already,' said Anne, her voice high and brittle, 'so for God's sake don't let go of me.'

'Don't worry,' said Zoe grimly, 'I won't let go. Come on.'

They edged their way round the rough walls of the cavern until they came to an opening in the rocky sides.

'Here we are,' said Zoe and relief flooded through her. 'Here's the passage.' Neither of them voiced the fear that haunted both; was it the right opening? Both following the glimmer from the torch hoping and praying that they were on the right track. As they stumbled uncertainly through the almost total darkness, Zoe kept up a flow of chatter, trying to reassure herself as much as Anne.

'I'm sure this is right, don't you remember that jutting rock? We passed this steep bit, I'm sure. This looks like the stone staircase we came down.'

But it was not and gradually both knew it. If they had been in the right passage they would have been back in the cellar by now. The torch finally expired and the thick darkness crowded round them. Zoe could hear Anne weeping and felt the tears pricking her own eyes. She spoke softly but firmly.

'Pull yourself together, Anne, we've got to think. We can't just stand here in the pitch black and let panic take over.' Anne continued sobbing and Zoe said, 'Come on, Anne. We must make a decision. Whichever way we go it'll be dark — do we go on and hope this passageway leads somewhere or do we go back to that cave place and try the next passage?'

'I don't know. It's so dark, I can't think straight.' Suddenly she gave a scream. 'What's that? Something against my legs. It's a rat!'

Then Zoe began to laugh, uncontrollably laughing and crying at the same time.

'Zoe! Zoe! Stop it!' Anne was nearly hysterical herself. 'Be quiet, Zoe!'

'It's all right, Anne, it's all right. It's Barney, not a rat. It's Barney. He'll show us the way out.'

Clutching a very licky Barney between them, both girls sat on the rocky floor of the passageway and laughed and cried until their fear was spent. Zoe untied the scarf round her hair and knotted it through Barney's collar; then holding hands they let the dog lead the way along the passage. To their surprise he did not take them back the way they had come, but continued along the path they had been following.

'Are you sure he knows the way?' asked Anne, her fear returning. 'This isn't the way we came.'

'Dogs have an uncanny sense of direction,' said Zoe, 'you said that yourself. Let's give him a chance. He may have found another way out.'

They followed the little dog further and further and as they went the passage narrowed and broadened, but the dog never faltered. Once the darkness was pierced by a faint beam of light and looking upwards they could see a round of daylight far above them.

'It's some sort of shaft,' said Zoe excitedly. 'A mine shaft, do you think?'

'I've no idea,' said Anne tiredly. 'It's like being at the bottom of a well.'

'Look out,' cried Zoe suddenly clutching her friend's arm and pulling her back against the wall of the passage.

'What's the matter?' Anne's voice shook with sudden fright.

'The shaft, or whatever it is goes on down; we're on a sort of ledge.' Straining to see in the faint light which filtered down, Anne looked where Zoe pointed and realised that the path narrowed until it was only about a yard wide and that there was a yawning hole beside them. She shut her eyes in horror and whispered with true reverence, 'Thank God, thank God you saw it, Zoe.'

Not taking their eyes from the hole and with their backs pressed firmly against the rough stone wall, they edged their way past the shaft and reached the next passage where they could touch the walls on both sides once more. Both of them stood for a moment weak with relief until Barney, who had crossed the ledge with sure-footed ease, pulled on the scarf-lead and whined. He continued his way into the enclosed corridor which led steeply uphill. Zoe tripped over something and cried out, letting go of the lead as she did so.

'Zoe,' called Anne anxiously into the darkness, 'are you all right?'

'Yes,' said Zoe, 'but I think I'm at the bottom of some steps.'

'Steps?'

'Yes,' she confirmed feeling in front of her with her hands. 'Come on Barney's found something.' Barney was whimpering and scratching at something at the top of the steps. Zoe felt blindly round her and using her hands as well as her feet, climbed the rough stone staircase until she reached the top. Barney was scratching on something ahead of them and reaching out Zoe found her fingers against solid wood.

'It's a door,' she breathed. 'Anne, it's a door.' She ran her hands over the rough wood and great metal hinges of a heavy old door. She searched for a handle and found a huge ring to lift the latch; but the door remained immovable.

'It's locked.' Her voice was dull with

disappointment.

'Bang on it,' cried Anne who had successfully negotiated the steps and was waiting in the darkness. She edged towards Zoe. 'Bang on it, someone might hear.'

Zoe began banging on the door with her fists, pounding against the thick wood in a desperate attempt to make somebody hear. But the sound she made seemed muffled in the darkness and who was there to hear anyway? But she kept hammering and she and Anne shouted at the tops of their voices. Barney joined in, barking happily, pleased to be part of what seemed to be a good game. Then Zoe cried out in pain. She had hit something hard and sharp. Exploring with her fingers she found an old iron bolt near the top of the door. She clutched at Anne.

'Anne, there's a bolt! Quickly, let's see if we can shift it.'

The bolt was very old and very stiff and hampered by the total darkness it took them some time to work it loose, but after several minutes it gradually eased and with a dull rusty scrape slid free. Zoe tried the heavy handle again. This time she felt the door give a little.

'It's moving,' she almost cried in relief.

'Push together,' said Anne and they both put their shoulders to the door. It was very stiff and the hinges creaked protestingly as inch by inch they forced it open. There was light the other side, no more than the faintest lightening in the darkness, but the realisation that they were at last emerging from the entombing passages gave them added strength and with one final effort they managed to open the door wide enough for each to squeeze through.

Zoe stared round her, her eyes gradually adjusting to the dim light. It was still very dark, but a faint grey light stealing through an opening a little further on, showed shapes around them, and Zoe guessed that they were in a windowless cellar connected to another.

'Come on,' she said, 'this way.' They stumbled towards the patch of grey light, trying not to fall over the refuse scattered on the floor, and reached a low archway leading to another cellar. This was lit by grey daylight filtering through a grimy window high up in the wall and festooned with cobwebs. It gave little enough light but for Zoe and Anne who had been so long in the dark it enabled them to see to a certain extent, and the fear engendered by the darkness began to ebb away.

'We're in a cellar,' said Anne. 'Look at all the junk that's stacked down here.' Round them were boxes and pieces of old furniture, some barrels and several piles of rubbish.

'Where do we go from here?' asked Anne pushing the hair out of her eyes with a grubby hand and leaving a smudge across her forehead. Glancing back into the first cellar, Zoe could not see the old door, cloaked in darkness, even though she knew exactly where to look.

'Come on,' called Anne, who was already halfway across the adjoining cellar, and Zoe turned away and followed her friend and Barney, picking their way across the accumulated rubbish in two more dingy cellars before they reached a flight of stone steps leading upward to a door. They paused at the bottom and Anne said, 'Whose house do you think we're in?'

'Haven't a clue,' replied Zoe, 'but there's only one way to find out; up we go, and just pray that this door isn't locked.'

10

The cellar door was not locked and Zoe and Anne came out into a stone-floored passageway. To the left it led to a huge kitchen and to the right it ended with a green baize door, normally cutting off the servants' quarters, but now standing open. In the distance they could hear a woman speaking and for a moment neither of them recognised the voice; it was harsh and angry.

'We told you there can be no further shipments at present as storage facilities have been withdrawn.' There was a pause which made it clear that the speaker was on the telephone, then she continued, 'That's not our problem. If you've been fool enough to bring the merchandise so near without checking as instructed, then you'll have to hold until we have reorganised this end.'

The receiver was replaced with a

clatter and Anne whispered, 'Come on, we must make ourselves known.' She strode ahead of Zoe who was now carrying a scrimmaging Barney and emerged from the passage into the sunlit hall of Shearwater House. She stopped short with a gasp to see Mrs. Penrose standing beside the telephone table staring out of the window.

Mrs. Penrose spun round, saying sharply, 'Who's there?' and stared in amazement to see Anne, Zoe and Barney, covered in smuts and cobwebs standing in her hall.

'What are you doing here?' Her voice was still abrupt and then as they came forward with their confusion of explanation, she relaxed into her usual good humour.

'My dears,' she cried holding up her hands to stem the tide, 'my dears, you sound as if you've had an awful experience. Now, before you say another word let me take you up to the bathroom so that you can tidy up and get comfortable, then you can tell me properly over a nice cup of tea. You both look as if you could do with one. Put the dog in the garden before you come up, Zoe dear. I'm so sorry I spoke sharply; you made me jump appearing from the kitchen like that. And,' she continued, as she led them upstairs to the bathroom, 'I'd just had a row with some business associate of James's. I wish they wouldn't bother him at home. He has a perfectly good office telephone and I'm always telling him, 'keep your work at the office, James, home is a place to relax in', but he never does — always working too hard. Now then, here are two clean towels. Take your time while I get Mrs. Croft to bring in tea.'

Prattling still, she left the bathroom and suddenly released from fear and swamped by the normality of Mrs. Penrose, Zoe and Anne dissolved into uncontrollable giggles. Zoe closed the bathroom door and they sat down on the soft pink carpet and laughed till the tears ran down their cheeks, carving runnels in the grime that covered them, and leaving them feeling quite weak. At length they went down to join Mrs. Penrose in the drawing room, feeling better for their wash, and their laughter.

James was there, too, and while he handed them the cups of tea his mother poured, Zoe explained more clearly what had happened. Even Mrs. Penrose did not interrupt as she told of the passageways which led under the cliff, prompted occasionally by Anne.

'And you say it comes up into our cellar?' said James incredulously. 'I must look into this.'

'But why?' said Mrs. Penrose.

'Why?'

'Yes, I mean why are these passageways here at all, and why do they link the cottage and the house?'

'I imagine they were used by smugglers in earlier times,' said James. 'It would be far easier to move goods undetected or hide them underground. The cottage and the house were built about the same time, remember, and they were troubled days. Lots of places had their built-in escape routes and hidey-holes.'

'But why haven't we found that old door before?' asked Mrs. Penrose.

'Because we've never really explored the cellars,' replied James. 'They're fairly extensive and we only use the outer one. I've never taken more than a cursory glance at the others.'

'And there's no window in the furthest one,' said Zoe. 'You can't see the door from across the cellar, I looked back and it was too dark. You could easily miss it even with a torch.'

'Obviously the passages are very old and somebody's rediscovered them, your end anyway, and has been using the way to the cliff to get into your underground room. Now you've discovered more passages, and there could be many more, perhaps part of an old mine. There used to be mines round here; I believe some even stretched out under the sea. If you go farther round the cliff you can see the old headgear, used for lowering the cage down the main shaft.'

'I didn't realise there were old mines round here,' said Anne. 'I never heard of any.'

'All worked out now,' replied James, 'but if they spread on to this part of the cliff it could explain the extent of these passages.'

'And that shaft,' said Zoe suddenly.

'Shaft?' James looked enquiring. 'What shaft?'

'When we were nearly at the cellar door we found ourselves at the bottom of a sort of shaft. We could see daylight at the top, couldn't we Anne? Perhaps that was an old mine shaft, but if so, it's not far from your house, James.'

'Good gracious,' twittered Mrs. Penrose, 'an open shaft! How very dangerous, James! We must find it and close it off at once. Somebody might fall in.'

'It would be a long fall,' said Anne. 'It was like being at the bottom of a well.'

'A well!' exclaimed James. 'We've an old well in the kitchen yard. It could make a perfect air hole for the underground passages. Excellent ventilation. You didn't have any problem breathing?'

Zoe shook her head. 'No, I never even thought about it.'

'If the well provided ventilation this end and the passages opened on to the cliffs the other the air would circulate freely. It's a good system. I really must investigate these underground passages; it's most intriguing.'

'The sooner it's sealed off the better,' said Mrs. Penrose with a nervous little laugh. 'Supposing these poor girls had been lost for ever in those catacombs — they might never have found their way out. It must be closed off at once.'

'Don't worry, Mother, I'll see to it all,' soothed James.

The mantelpiece clock chimed five.

'Heavens!' cried Anne. 'Look at the time. David'll be thinking I've crashed the car. I must fly.' She jumped to her feet and returned her empty teacup to Mrs. Penrose. 'I'm sorry to dash,' she said, 'but it's much later than I thought.'

Zoe got up, too. 'I must go as well,' she said. 'I'm really very sorry we burst in on you like this, Mrs. Penrose, I hope we didn't disturb your telephoning.' Mrs. Penrose looked up sharply before she smiled and said, 'Not at all dear, I told you it was only some tiresome clients of James's. You really must give them your office number only, James,' she added petulantly, turning to her son.

'Yes, Mother,' he agreed absently, then turning to Zoe and Anne said, 'I'll walk you back,' and without waiting for a reply he led the way to the front door.

As soon as they reached Shearwater Cottage, Anne clambered into her car and set off home, promising to come over and see Zoe in a day or two. 'But do come in for coffee when you're in the village,' she said, 'any time.' She bumped off down the track and Zoe turned back once more to the cottage. She could hardly believe that it was less than three hours since she had arrived with Anne and they had begun their exploration. Suddenly she realised that the doorway from the secret room into the passageways beyond would still be propped open. Now she found herself unwilling to venture back down there to close it again; and equally unwilling to leave it open.

'James,' she said and paused, she did not want him to think she was afraid.

'What?'

'Would you mind very much coming down to the cellar with me to close up the secret room and the door into the underground passages? It's just, well, just that Anne and I left it all propped open, so that we would be able to get back in again when we'd found Barney.' In spite of herself, she heard her voice tremble a little at the thought of Barney disappearing once again into the darkness.

'Of course,' said James. 'You needn't come down at all. I'll shut it again and you can lock the upstairs door and feel quite safe.'

'Thank you very much,' said Zoe with real gratitude and led him into the house. She kept a firm hold on Barney until James reappeared and locked the cellar door behind him.

'There you are,' he said cheerfully. 'All locked up again. It's an interesting room. How did you manage to open the second door? Once I'd let it swing shut, I couldn't see how to open it again.'

'That's something that puzzles me,' said Zoe. 'We found the entrance by tapping the walls, why didn't Jarvis do the same?'

'Perhaps he assumed that he'd come in by the door,' said James. 'You found the entrance because you knew there was one, but if you'd been brought to a dark room through dark passages, you might not have realised there were two entrances.'

'I suppose so,' said Zoe leading the way into the sitting room and flopping into a chair. James sat down as well and looked across at her earnestly.

'I think it would be a good idea if you

put that great bookcase back over the door to the secret room,' he said. 'It would be safer if it were completely blocked off. You don't want any unfortunate accidents with people getting shut into those passages beyond.'

Zoe looked surprised. 'People?' she said. 'What people? No one's going into my cellar.'

'No, probably not,' agreed James easily, 'but having all that exposed down there might, well, make the cottage more difficult to sell. After all, it's a bit gruesome when you come to think of it.' Zoe, who had been making determined efforts not to think of it in those terms had to agree, but added, 'It won't matter about being a bad selling point through, because I've decided not to sell.'

'Not sell?' James looked at her enquiringly. 'Why not? I thought you wanted a quick sale so you could dive off back to London.'

'I'm not going back to London.'

'Not going back?'

'Well, not yet anyway, I've decided to stay down her for a while. Circumstances have altered and so I'm going to stay.'

'I see,' said James. 'We'll be delighted you're staying, of course, but what are you going to do down here? There aren't many jobs about, it's all very countrified.'

'I've already arranged a job,' said Zoe, 'and so I'll be here for the next few months anyway.'

'Hmm,' said James, 'then you'll forgive me for saying that you certainly ought to have that room permanently sealed off; bricked up. I'm certain you couldn't be comfortable here knowing there was only an old door between you and the room where that man died. Have it bricked up and forget about it.'

'You're probably right,' agreed Zoe, suddenly too tired to argue. 'I should be more comfortable with no way in there any more.'

'Like sealing up a tomb,' said James, and Zoe wished he had not.

'I know a builder who'll do it for you,' James went on, 'I'll fix it up for you if you like. Leave it to me and in a day or two when he's done the job, you'll have nothing to worry about at all. In the meantime, just keep the cellar door locked and you can forget everything and begin to enjoy living here in Port Marsden.'

Zoe wondered if she would ever be able to 'forget everything', but she did not say so, she just thanked James and said she would be very grateful if he would ask the builder to come as soon as possible.

'Mother will be delighted you're staying here for a while,' James said as he took his leave, 'and don't worry, we'll soon have that doorway bricked up then you can be comfortable.' With a brief wave he set off home to tell his mother the news, and Zoe closed the door, unaware of the consternation that news had caused him.

11

There was a light covering of mist early on Wednesday morning as Zoe slid into the driving seat of the Mini and with Barney beside her and her overnight case on the back seat, set off to London to tie off, once and for all, the loose ends of her life there. She had spent the previous day quietly organising herself in the cottage and making a list of all the things she had to do while she was in London. The cellar door was still locked and she was determined that it should remain so until James's man came to brick up the doorway into the secret room.

Stopping only for coffee once on the M4, Zoe drove into London soon after two o'clock and went straight to the office. Leaving her car in the underground car park she took the lift up to the fifth floor and pausing for a moment to gather her courage protectively round her, stepped out into the office.

It was almost an anti-climax; everything looked the same, familiar and yet somehow much smaller. One of the typists looked up in surprise.

'Zoe! I thought you were on holiday.'

'I have been,' said Zoe, 'I still am, but I've come in to see Mr. Stackton.'

The girl glanced at the closed door that led first to Zoe's own office and then through to Robert's.

'Does he know you're coming?'

'Indeed he does,' said Zoe crisply, and crossed the room to go into her office.

'Rosemary's in there,' said the other girl hastily. Zoe turned. 'In my office or in his?'

'She's been doing your job while you've been away.' The girl sounded apologetic, 'You know she's engaged to Mr. Stackton.'

'I did hear, yes,' said Zoe and went through to her office, closing the door softly behind her.

Rosemary was seated at Zoe's desk typing on Zoe's typewriter. She gave Zoe no more than a glance and said, 'You can go in, he's expecting you.' Zoe's prepared congratulations died on her lips and she merely nodded and knocking on Robert's door went in. Robert rose to his feet at once and said, 'Zoe, how nice to see you! Do come in and close the door.' He spoke as if to an acquaintance he had not seen for several years rather than to the personal assistant who had shared his struggles and his triumphs as he had set up and established his company. He showed her to a seat as if she were a client rather than one of his staff and offered her a cigarette although he knew she had never smoked.

Zoe felt quite detached, as if she were watching as an outsider. She studied Robert. He looked as he had always looked and yet there was a difference. His manner was entirely false, jovial, which he had never been, and hearty. It was clear he must have known how she felt about him or been made aware by someone, and the comfortable companionship with which they had worked together and the ease with which they had been able to talk, had gone, leaving only awkwardness which Robert tried to cover with bluff good humour and Zoe escaped by retreating into chilly politeness tinged with asperity.

'Having a good holiday down there at your cottage? Always thought a holiday cottage might be nice.'

'Very nice, thank you. It always breaks the monotony to find a dead body in the cellar.'

'Sounded like a very nasty business that,' Robert said, and then before she could reply, went on, 'Still, I expect that's all sorted out now and you can relax again. Sorry you'll be leaving us when your holiday's over, we've had some good times together. You've done a lot for the company and I'm grateful, but I quite understand that you want a change. I've written you a testimonial.'

He buzzed the intercom and said, 'Rosemary, bring in Zoe's testimonial, please,' then he went on, 'but of course if you ever need a reference or a referee don't hesitate to give my name.' Rosemary came in carrying a sheet of paper which she put in front of Robert before standing behind his chair, a proprietorial hand resting on his shoulder. Robert handed Zoe the paper which she put into her handbag without so much as a glance. She stood up and said, 'I'll go and clear my desk. I left several things there when I went away.'

'Don't worry,' said Rosemary. 'I did it for you. When we heard you had decided to leave I took over your job until we can find a replacement and of course I couldn't work with all your bits and pieces in the drawers. They're in my office in a cardboard box.' Zoe was dumbstruck and even Robert had the grace to look embarrassed at Rosemary's precipitate action.

'Rosemary, that was a little unnecessary, you knew Zoe was coming in to do it today,' he pointed out. But Rosemary was unrepentant.

'Well, I've saved her a job then. I'm sure she's in a hurry. Now, Robert, don't be cross, I was only trying to help.'

This last remark was said caressingly and to Zoe it was the end.

'Thank you for my testimonial, Robert, I'll collect my cardboard box on the way out,' and turning on her heel she stalked out leaving Robert to say, 'Now, Rosy, you shouldn't have talked to her like that,' and Rosemary to remark, 'Silly, prissy little thing.'

Zoe picked up the cardboard box from the desk and glanced in at its contents: a few letters, a box of tissues, some newspaper cuttings mostly about Robert and the company and a library book; all that was left of her life in that office. She was just going into the outer office when she noticed the rubber plant Robert had given her at Christmas. She had called it Ron and taken great care of it, bathing its leaves in milk so that they gleamed darkly green. On impulse she picked it up and pausing in the outer office said to the typist there, 'You can tell Rosemary I took my rubber plant as well. She'll have to get one of her own.'

The girl nodded and said, 'Right, I'll tell her. Oh, by the way, Zoe, do you want to contribute to the present?'

'Present?'

'Yes, we're all contributing to buy Mr. Stackton and Rosemary a wedding present.'

'No, thank you,' said Zoe. 'I shan't be giving anything. Goodbye.' And she headed for the lift clutching her box and Ron the rubber plant knowing that she had been petty over the present, but feeling far better for being so.

As she drove away from the office and out along the Embankment Zoe found herself reliving the last half-hour. She realised quite definitely that she had been right to give up the job. There was no way that she could have continued to work for Robert with

Rosemary queening it about the office. Robert, too, had changed, was somehow diminished and might not revert to his usual cool-headed self with Rosemary apparently able to tell him what to do. Zoe found she was shaking with anger at the thought of Rosemary going through the drawers of her desk. She did not keep anything particularly private there, there was always too much to be done to bother with personal things at work, but it was Rosemary's intrusion where she had no right which made Zoe so angry. Glancing sideways and seeing Ron reposing gracefully on the passenger seat made her give a bitter smile. 'And I hope the one he buys her shrivels up and dies,' she said viciously. Barney, relegated to the back of the car beside the suitcase, blew encouragingly in her ear when he heard her voice and his affection made her want to cry.

'But he's not the Robert I loved,' Zoe said to the dog. 'She's changed him already and by the time they've been

married ten years he'll be unrecognis-
able.' But the thought did not comfort
her much and she was glad when at last
she pulled up in front of the stark
Victorian house in which she had the
ground floor flat; there was so much to
do there that she would have no further
time for thought. Her rent was paid
until the end of the month, so she had
only to write a letter to her landlady
and say she was going. This she did at
once, leaving her new address for any
outstanding bills, and having posted it
in the pillar box on the corner she set to
work clearing the flat. None of the
furniture was hers, but she had added
some of her own china, a rug or two,
cushions, pictures, and some more
cheerful curtains in the living room.
Room by room she removed her
belongings only leaving the sheets on
the bed till the morning. She ate tinned
food from the larder and packed all the
rest of her stores into two cardboard
boxes to transfer them to the cottage
pantry. At last everything was packed

up and standing in the hall ready to go in the car next day.

Zoe flopped into an armchair feeling exhausted. The room round her looked cold and impersonal stripped of its ornaments and suddenly she longed to be out and away from it. For a moment she was tempted to load up and set off for Cornwall at once, but common sense prevailed; she knew she was too tired to drive through the night and so she decided to go to bed now and make an early start in the morning.

The silence round her was suddenly shattered by the telephone. It's shrillness jerked her to her feet and she picked up the receiver.

'Hello?'

'Hello, Zoe, is that you? It's me, Greg.'

'Greg!' Zoe was surprised to hear him and yet pleased to hear a friendly voice.

'Everything all right up there?'

'Yes, of course,' said Zoe. 'Is everything all right down there? Why are you ringing?'

'Well, I called round earlier this evening with some news for you but you weren't there and the place looked all shut up; then I remembered you'd said you were going to London to sort a few things out, so I thought I'd give you a call.'

'How did you know my number?'

'You gave it to me when you instructed me to sell the cottage. And that's what I'm ringing about. I've had a very good offer for the cottage.'

'But I don't want to sell anymore.'

'No, I know, but before I refused and said that Shearwater Cottage was off the market I wanted to be sure. I mean, your trip to London might have changed your mind again.'

'Oh, I see. Well, it hasn't. I still don't want to sell.'

'Sure?'

'Sure.' Zoe spoke with a new certainty. Her day in London had had quite the opposite effect; she had felt strangely claustrophobic in the offices of Amalgamated Chemicals and in the familiar bustle of the city crowds she had felt stifled and solitary and longed for the fresh sea breeze blowing across the cliff.

'I'm leaving first thing in the morning and shall take it steadily. I should be back by early evening. The car'll be so loaded its bottom'll probably drag along the road.' She heard Greg laugh and felt comforted by the sound.

'Well, do take it steady, we want you back in one piece. How would it be if I brought some food up to Shearwater and we had dinner together? I'll cook.'

'That sounds lovely,' said Zoe, surprised but pleased by his offer. It would be so much more welcoming not to be alone on her first evening home. 'Lovely.'

'Good,' said Gregory simply. 'See you tomorrow evening then. Take care.'

'I will. See you.' The phone clicked and Zoe replaced the receiver. It was comforting to know someone was thinking of her. Her gaze travelled round the shabby room and she thought, I'm glad I'm leaving this, and she crossed into the bedroom to spend her last night there before she took Anne's advice to 'cut loose and start again'.

12

Gregory stood in the porch of Shearwater Cottage with a box of food at his feet and a bottle of wine under his arm. As Zoe drew up outside he came to open the car door for her and help her out. It had been a long drive and she felt stiff. Barney leapt across her seat, glad to be out of the car and eager to take possession of his territory once again.

'Welcome home,' said Greg as Zoe stretched to ease her stiffness. He smiled and she smiled tiredly back at him as she said, 'Thank you, it's good to be home.'

'You really are loaded,' said Greg, peering in through the car windows. 'What on earth's that?' He pointed to the rubber plant standing on the back floor of the car, its green leaves carefully interspersed with the rest of the luggage so that they would not get damaged.

'That's Ron, my rubber plant.' said Zoe seriously. She handed Gregory the key to the house and said, 'Will you open up and we can start to get all this stuff indoors?' Greg did as she asked and carried the provisions he had bought into the kitchen before he came out to help Zoe. When he did emerge it was to find suitcases and boxes stacked beside the car and Ron standing aloof waiting to be installed somewhere suitable.

'Now then,' said Greg once they had moved everything indoors, 'leave all your unpacking until tomorrow and sit down with a drink while I cook dinner. What will you have? I've brought gin and tonic, whisky and ginger or wine.'

Zoe laughed. 'You have come well prepared! I'd like a whisky, please, well topped up with ginger.'

Gregory poured them each a drink and then said, 'Now you sit there and unwind after your drive and I'll get on with the meal.'

'Oh, really, I can cook the meal,' protested Zoe.

'Certainly not, part of the deal was that I'd do it. Let's face it, I'm not attempting anything too difficult. How do you like your steak?'

'Medium rare,' replied Zoe.

'Medium rare it is.'

'But I'm not going to sit here by myself while you're slaving away in the kitchen. Can't I come out and talk to you while you cook?'

'Yes,' said Greg, 'provided you don't interfere.'

'Promise,' said Zoe.

While Greg grilled the steak and fried up chips, onions and mushrooms, Zoe told him about cleaning out the flat. She mentioned the office, too, but did not describe the half hour she had spent there. She wondered if Gregory had discovered from Anne her real reason for leaving London and settling permanently in Port Marsden. He did not ask and accepted without question the edited version of her day in London.

As they sat down to eat, Greg said casually, 'You had a visitor yesterday.'

'A visitor?'

'Yes, when I came up to tell you about that offer for the cottage a van drove away.'

'Who was it? Do you know?'

'No one I knew. Were you expecting anyone?'

'No, unless James Penrose had already got someone to do the bricking up, not realising I was away. I can't remember if I told him I was going or not.'

'Bricking up?'

'Yes, he suggested I should have the entrance to the secret room bricked up, so that I could forget it was there and the entrance to all those underground passages would be closed.'

'I heard you and Anne went exploring them,' said Greg. 'You must have been mad, both of you, wandering off in there on your own.' He spoke quite sharply and immediately Zoe was on the defensive.

'We didn't wander off on purpose. Barney disappeared into them before I could stop him. He didn't come back when I called and I was afraid he was lost. I couldn't just leave him.'

'With the result it was you who nearly got lost. David was pretty cross with Anne, I gathered. He's made her promise never to go down there again. You won't go into those passages again either, will you?'

Zoe shuddered. 'I have no intention of doing so, that's why I'm having it all blocked up, no more accidents.'

'I'm glad to hear it,' said Greg, once again turning his attention to his plate. Zoe watched him for a moment and then said, 'Who told you about our adventure anyway?'

'Anne, of course,' replied Greg. 'I bumped into her in the square yesterday. It's only melon for pud, I'm afraid. I hope you like it.'

'One of my favourites,' said Zoe. She took a deep breath and continued, 'it's kind of you to take so much trouble, Greg. Why did you?'

'No trouble at all, why shouldn't I? I didn't think you'd be in the mood for cooking after driving down from London.'

Zoe smiled at him and said, 'You were right, thank you very much,' but inside she wondered again how much more Anne had told him when he had bumped into her in the square.

Filling the silence which fell between them, Zoe said, 'Who wanted to buy the cottage?'

'I'm not sure,' Greg answered, 'it was all a little odd really, it was someone working through an agent. He offered the full asking price, but wanted an early completion; just the sort of offer you wanted last week. That's why I phoned, to be sure you really didn't want to sell.'

'But do you think it was someone you'd brought out to see the place?' asked Zoe.

'I don't know. He was as I said, working through an agent, but he didn't want to view, just said the property was known to his principal and they wanted a quick sale.'

'Well, he's too late' said Zoe. 'I'm sorry if it's put you in an awkward position.'

'It hasn't,' said Greg cheerfully. 'People are always changing their minds in this business, it's part of the job.' 'You know,' he remarked as they sat drinking coffee, 'if you're going to be here permanently you ought to have a phone put in. I don't like the thought of you alone up here without one. You're a bit in the wilds, you know.'

'Aunt Jessie managed without one, and she was elderly as well as alone,' said Zoe.

'I know, but it doesn't mean that you have to.'

'Well, I'll think about it,' said Zoe. 'Quite a lot of things need to be organised. It probably would be a good idea. More coffee?'

Gregory did not stay late and as soon as he had roared away into the warm summer darkness Zoe went to bed. Immediately she fell into a deep, dreamless sleep, but she was jerked awake some time later by Barney. He had elected to sleep on the landing and suddenly he began to bark. Rushing downstairs he barked furiously demanding to be let out into the garden. After a moment's haziness Zoe came fully awake; slipping out of bed and without turning on a light she lifted the corner of one of the curtains. The midnight darkness enclosed the cottage and was complete. There was no moon and no other light to illuminate the garden. All was apparently still and quiet, but Barney remained downstairs whining and scratching at the back door. Safe in the knowledge that all doors and windows were securely fastened including the cellar door Zoe decided to do nothing. She would stay where she was, upstairs in bed.

'Pull yourself together,' she whispered aloud, 'it's probably only a fox that's disturbed him. No one else'd be out there at this time of night.' Resolutely she climbed back into bed and made determined efforts to go back to sleep. Barney padded back up the stairs at last satisfied that whatever, or whoever, it was outside had gone, and settled down once more on the landing. He slept at once with one ear cocked for future disturbances. There were none and at last Zoe, too, drifted back into uneasy sleep. Next morning, in comforting daylight, Zoe was able to convince herself that there was nothing to worry about and that Barney must have heard an animal in the garden. She had a leisurely breakfast looking out across the cliffs to the sea beyond. It was a view she had already come to love, one continually changing in mood and colour, altered by the wind, the clouds and the sun so that it was never quite the same twice, yet always the same in essence; the same as it had been since the cottage was built and before. It would be there always, varied by the seasons, and Zoe was glad.

She spent the rest of the morning busily sorting out all the things she had brought down from the flat. Ron was ensconced in a corner of the living room, his leaves newly bathed, and his old flower pot smartly covered by one of Aunt Jessie's brass plant pots; familiar rugs on the floor and favourite ornaments on the mantel made Zoe feel more settled and she looked round the room with affection.

Just before lunch she heard Barney barking and looking out through the window she saw James's car had drawn up outside and noticed with a slight sinking of her heart that Mrs. Penrose was clambering out of the passenger seat. Zoe greeted them at the front door.

'Zoe, my dear,' cried Mrs. Penrose from halfway up the path, 'I do hope you don't mind us dropping in. You've been out the last once or twice we've called.'

'I'm sorry,' said Zoe politely, standing aside for them to come into the cottage. 'I went up to London to collect the last of my things.'

'Well, haven't you made it look charming,' said Mrs. Penrose looking round, 'so much more your own with your own bits and pieces about.'

'I've organised a builder for you,' said James coming straight to the point of his visit. 'He'll be over to see you to have a look at the job. His name's Spring, he works for one of the big firms but he sometimes takes on odd jobs like this on his own account. He'll be up to see you sometime soon.'

'He may have been. Greg saw a van drive off when he came up the other day. Do you know, somebody's made an offer for the cottage? Funny, isn't it? I'd have snapped it up last week.'

'Are you sure you don't want to anyway?' asked Mrs. Penrose. 'If it's a good offer you could always buy somewhere else, not so cut off. I wouldn't be happy living here alone.

I should be terrified at night; you never know who might be prowling around.'

'Now stop that, Mother' said James severely. 'You mustn't go putting your fears into Zoe's head or she'll start hearing noises at night.'

Zoe remembering the disturbance in the night said, casually, 'Barney heard something last night actually. I expect it was a fox or something. It made him bark anyway.'

'My dear, I should have been petrified,' cried Mrs. Penrose. 'I don't know how you can live here alone, a young girl by herself. It's not right, is it, James?' But before he could reply she went on, 'After all, think what was going on in your cellar, and you here all alone.'

Zoe, wishing Mrs. Penrose would be quiet, managed a shaky laugh and said, 'But that's all finished now and with both ends of the passage blocked there'll be no danger there.'

Mrs. Penrose still looked dubious, but James said briskly, 'Of course not.

Come along, Mother, we must go home for lunch. Spring'll be up to see you again soon, and he'll probably do the job over the weekend.'

Zoe thanked them for coming to tell her about the builder.

'I'm sorry you had to come over, but with no telephone it's always more difficult to arrange things. I'm thinking of having one put in now I'm going to live here.'

'Good idea,' said James as he helped Mrs. Penrose into the car. 'Don't you think so, Mother?'

'I do indeed,' said Mrs. Penrose. 'I'm sure you won't feel quite comfortable here until you have a link with the outside world.'

'Don't go on like that, Mother,' said James in exasperation. 'It is a good idea, Zoe, though you may find you have trouble getting them to put one in. I understand there's a long waiting list in this area. We had a long wait for a number even though we already had a line in.'

'Then I'll get on and apply at once' said Zoe cheerfully, thinking what a pair of pessimists the Penroses were. She said as much to David and Anne Campion over the supper table at the vicarage later that evening. Anne had appeared towards the end of the afternoon and carried Zoe off to spend the evening with them and Zoe, tired of her own company, went willingly.

'It's kindly intended,' said David. 'Mrs. Penrose is obviously worried about you alone in the cottage and you must admit quite a lot of disturbing things have gone on since you first came down. She used to go across and see your aunt, too, you know. She means well.'

'You're too charitable, darling,' said Anne. 'There are times when she's downright nosey. She's always checking up on what people are doing.'

'Well, I don't mind really,' said Zoe with a laugh, 'but I think I'll take James's advice and get an application for a phone in as soon as possible.'

'I quite agree with that,' said Anne, 'then any of us can give you a ring instead of trailing out to see you. When do you start work, by the way?'

'I'm going over to see Mr. Enodoc on Monday and I'll take it from there,' replied Zoe. 'I'm looking forward to getting started. It's funny, but I'm so used to a daily routine that I don't feel quite right without one.'

'You haven't had much of a holiday,' said David. 'With one thing and another I'd have thought you'd want to have another week or two to yourself before getting tied down to work again.'

Zoe shook her head.

'It's a new life and I can't wait to begin it,' she said. 'And I don't want time to brood.' David nodded. He understood as well as Anne, who in the cosiness of the kitchen earlier had heard about Zoe's trip to London and her meeting with Robert and Rosemary. However, he mentioned the escapade in the catacombs while Anne fetched coffee, sounding worried as he said, 'I was horrified to hear what had happened to you, wandering lost in those passages. It could so easily have ended in tragedy, you know.' Zoe reassured him by telling him about the arrangements James had made to close off the cellar room and he looked relieved, but said no more as Anne returned with the coffee tray.

Later on as he drove Zoe home to Shearwater Cottage he said, 'I think you arc very brave, Zoe, and determined. Your determination'll see you through this unhappiness and you'll find someone who can return all the love you have to offer and when you do, you'll find that love returned is an entirely different emotion from any one-sided feeling you may have experienced so far.'

Zoe, a little selfconsciously said, 'Thank you, David.'

He laughed and said, 'Sermon over! Here we are. Barney sounds pleased to see you.'

When David had driven away into

the darkness Zoe let Barney out of the front door to let him have a final run in the garden while she checked the doors and windows for the night. They were all latched and locked. Barney came in and settled happily on the landing while Zoe had a long bath before going to bed. She lay in the hot water and thought about the new life on which she was embarking. It was incredible to think that this time two weeks ago, or even one week ago, she had been planning to sell the cottage and go back to her little flat and the familiar offices of Amalgamated Chemicals. Even her friends had changed. Before all her social life had somehow tied in with the office. She had a few other acquaintances in London, with no family and having lost touch with all her school friends, there was hardly anyone with whom she could claim actual friendship. And yet since that first visit to Port Marsden to see her inheritance, she had come to know several people better than any in London.

She thought of them now with affection, the Campions so hospitable and understanding, Gregory Enodoc and his father, both charming and good company, James Penrose and his mother, both so anxious to help. She had to admit that she found Mrs. Penrose very irritating and there was something about James that made her feel rather uncomfortable when she was with him, but she knew David Campion was right, they meant well, were trying to offer a friendly hand and make her feel welcome.

Barney started to bark.

13

She heard him scuttle downstairs still barking furiously and leapt out of the bath. Struggling into her bath robe Zoe opened the bathroom door and listened. She could hear nothing but Barney's continued barking, but her body hot from the bath became clammy with cold fear. She peered down the staircase; below the lights were still on, because she had intended to go and make a hot drink after she had had her bath.

'Quiet, Barney,' she called as he still danced round the front door. Suddenly her heart missed a beat. The front door! Had she locked it when Barney had come in from the garden? It could still be unlocked, an intruder could get in if it was still on the latch. A sudden panic, increased by Barney's continued noise, welled up inside her and she ran, stumbling, almost falling down the stairs and flinging herself against the front door, slammed the heavy bolts home. For a moment she leant against the door her heart pounding, then she dropped on her knees beside Barney and clutching him to her calmed him down a little so that at least he stopped barking, though he remained alert with his ears cocked.

'There's no one there,' Zoe told herself reassuringly. 'Why on earth would anyone want to come here at this time of night?' She spoke aloud and the sound of her own voice calmed her a little. 'It's obvious the house is occupied and that I haven't gone to bed and that there's a dog here. A prowler would know he was on to a loser here, don't you think so, Barney? Barney! Whatever is the matter?' For Barney had rushed over to one of the living room windows and started to bark again.

Taking her courage firmly in hand, Zoe crossed to the window and said loudly 'Quiet, Barney, there's no one there.'

But she was wrong. As she approached the uncurtained window a face appeared and for what seemed eternity pressed itself open-mouthed against the pane. And yet it was not a normal human face, sharp featured, with hair framing it, but was strangely flat and distorted, smooth on top like an egg.

As she saw it Zoe let out a piercing scream and her hands flew to her face as if to fend off the fear. The face did not seem to react to her scream, but kept moving from side to side as if grinding its nose into the window. For a few seconds Zoe stared in horror at the grotesque form while Barney barked continuously at it, then with sudden supreme effort she rushed to the window and jerked the curtains across covering the face outside; then round the room pulling the curtains at every window, then the same in the kitchen so that the night and its prowler were shut out. Automatically she checked the cellar door and at last feeling as secure as she could make herself she went back into the sitting room. For a moment there was silence, Barney stood, his head on one side, listening and Zoe listened, too.

As her mind went back over the dreadful moment when the face had appeared she found she had taken in more than she had realised. In spite of her fear, first at the arrival of the face, and then at its hideous appearance as it postured against the window, she knew on calmer reflection that it had merely been a man with a stocking pulled down over his head to hide his features. He must have been wearing black to blend with the darkness so that in the light from the room only his face was visible. A burglar? It must have been someone hoping for easy pickings from an isolated house. He was probably going to wait until the lights went out before trying to break in, but Barney had heard him.

Perhaps it was a peeping Tom;

someone who knew a girl lived out here alone and had come out hoping to catch a glimpse of her in an unguarded moment; or even worse than someone merely peeping. Zoe flopped into a chair her heart pounding again, as she thought of the unlocked front door. He could so easily have let himself in while she was in the bath. Except for Barney. Zoe felt very cold and suddenly realised she was still clad only in her bath robe. Well, if that's what the prowler had come to see he had had something from his visit. Zoe shuddered and wished her phone was already installed. She wondered fleetingly if she should make a dash for the car and take sanctuary at the vicarage, but the thought of opening the door and crossing the garden in darkness which concealed the owner of the face was more terrifying than staying behind barred doors.

Barney now lay down, relaxed on the floor and Zoe thought that the intruder whoever it was must have gone. If he were still in the garden Barney would not have settled again.

'Thank goodness I've got you, Barney,' said Zoe reaching down to stroke the little dog at her feet. Barney thumped his tail. 'You saw him off, didn't you? I couldn't let you out though. However brave you are, a quick boot in the ribs would be the end of you.' So saying, she forced herself to go back to her bedroom.

Although the curtains were now all closely drawn Zoe decided to leave a light on downstairs so that if she needed to come down again in the night, she would not have to stumble down in the dark, nor wonder what it might conceal. Upstairs she quickly fastened all the windows and drew the curtains against further intrusion and content at last there was nothing further she could do, she got into bed where she tossed and turned, drifting in and out of sleep until morning came and the fears of the night retreated.

As soon as she had breakfasted Zoe went outside. On the flowerbed under the window were two deep footmarks, showing where the prowler had stood as he peered in. Relieved to find hard evidence of his visit Zoe drove into Port Marsden to report the incident to the police.

The police house was set in a well-tended garden on one of the steep hills which ran up from the harbour square. The panda car was parked in the driveway and P.C. Dewar was in his office. He took Zoe in and sat her down in a chair and then returning to his desk listened, uninterrupting, as she related the events of the previous night.

'What I don't understand is what he wanted,' Zoe said when she had told him the facts. 'I mean, the man before, the man we thought was a burglar was trying to reach the convict in the cellar, but this man can't have been.'

'Probably only a peeping Tom,' said P.C. Dewar calmly.

'Only!' exclaimed Zoe.

'I agree it was very frightening for you, being out there alone,' said P.C.

Dewar, 'but he probably only wanted to look, not to harm you. Don't worry, we'll keep a particular eye on your cottage at night and see if we can pick him up. We'll start tonight. It's funny though, we've had no other complaints about a prowler. Do remember to keep your curtains drawn at night, won't you, so's not to encourage him.'

'Encourage him!' Zoe was angry.

'Well, put it this way, if he knows you're alone and you don't bother to draw your curtains, particularly upstairs, it may tempt him to come visiting again.'

'Don't worry, he'll get no second chance.'

'Good,' said P.C. Dewar, 'and don't worry, we'll be about during the night. Now if you'll sign your statement. And I'd take steps to get a phone in if you're intending to stay there.'

Zoe left the police station and went down to the post office on the square to find out how to apply for a telephone. She lingered for a moment by the harbour wall watching the gulls scavenging round the moored fishing boats.

It was another fine day and the sun shone down from a clear sky, sparkling the water, enveloping the harbour in yellow warmth. The sea, smooth and calm, gentled the fishing boats at their moorings and slapped quietly against the harbour wall. Along the sides of the harbour the faded colour-washed houses peered expectantly out across the water and despite the fact that she was standing at the heart of the village with life going on busily behind her in the square, Zoe was aware of marvellous tranquility, a soothing quietness and was glad for the time to be part of it. Gone from her life was the hassle of London and in its place was the quiet busyness of Port Marsden.

'Why, it's Zoe. How are you, my dear?' Mrs. Penrose's effusive tones cut through her reverie and brought Zoe sharply back to reality. She sighed inwardly and said, 'Fine thank you.'

James and Mrs. Penrose had crossed the square to speak to her and determined not to let her escape now,

Mrs. Penrose went on, 'You're just the person I want to see. Now that you'll be here for the church's patronal festival, the Michaelmas fête, held at our house you know, I'm sure you'd love to help; even take a stall perhaps.'

A little taken aback by this Zoe stammered, 'Well, I don't know, I mean I'm not really settled yet. I'll help of course, but I'm very much the newcomer. I wouldn't want to interfere.'

'My dear girl, we need every pair of hands we can get. It'll be marvellous if you join us. I'll tell Anne that you've agreed and she'll let you know what we want you to do.'

'Now, Mother,' said James severely, 'stop pushing Zoe into doing things she doesn't want to. She's had a hard couple of weeks.'

Mrs. Penrose began to say that she was not pushing Zoe into anything when she stopped and said, 'You're looking rather peaky, dear, are you overtired? Not sleeping well?'

'I am a bit tired,' admitted Zoe and

she told them about the prowler.

'Of course when he'd gone I did go to bed, but I didn't really sleep; I was listening to hear if he came back. Silly, because Barney would have barked if he had.'

'Brave dog,' cooed Mrs. Penrose, 'and brave girl, too. I'd have been petrified if I'd seen a face at my window. Now I know there's a peeping Tom about I shall draw the curtains the moment it begins to get dark. You're so cut off there, all alone.' Mrs. Penrose shuddered.

'Now, Mother,' said James again, 'don't start on all that. You'll have Zoe too scared to live there soon and she's only just moved in.'

'I know, that's why I'm worried. I mean it's still summer now, but imagine in the winter, dark before she gets home. She'll have to let herself into a dark house, always wondering if this man has come back; is waiting inside.'

'Stop it, Mother,' James said sharply. 'If you frighten her away she won't be there to help with your precious fête.'

The mention of the fête diverted Mrs. Penrose, for which Zoe was grateful, and promising to offer Anne her help, Zoe escaped to her car. It was only as she turned into the track to the cottage that she remembered she had done nothing about the telephone. About to turn round at once and return to the post office she changed her mind as she caught sight of a car outside her house. As she drove up behind it a man in blue overalls got out.

'Miss Carson? I'm Graham Spring. Mr. Penrose asked me to call.'

'Oh, yes,' said Zoe relieved. 'I am pleased to see you, Mr. Spring. Just a minute, I'll let us in.' She opened the door and Barney exploded out to welcome them. Graham Spring fended him off and followed Zoe into the house. She led the way into the kitchen.

'Did Mr. Penrose tell you what has to be done?'

'Bit of brickwork in the cellar.'

'That's right. I'll show you.' Zoe

turned the key in the cellar door and they went down the steps.

Mr. Spring looked at the doorway. 'That shouldn't take me long,' he said. 'If I build on the inside of the door we can just close it against the wall.'

'You mean the door will open on to a blank wall.'

'That'll be the easiest if that's all right with you.'

'That'll be fine,' said Zoe edging towards the steps again. She longed to be out of the dingy cellar and knew she would always dislike it down there.

'Be round tomorrow then,' said Mr. Spring, 'in the afternoon when I've finished work on the site.'

Zoe carefully locked the cellar door behind them and showed Mr. Spring out.

'I shall be glad when the job's done,' she said. 'Do I have to get any materials for you?'

'No, no. Don't worry about that,' he replied. 'I'll get what I need and put it all in the price.'

Glad to have at least one of her problems well on the way to being settled, Zoe had a quick omelette for lunch and drove over to see Mr. Enodoc at Charfield Manor.

14

Gregory's father was delighted to see her. As she pulled up outside the great front door Zoe saw him coming round the side of the house carrying a tray full of French beans. He peered towards the Mini, uncertain for a moment as to who was in it, but as Zoe got out and he recognised her, his face split in to a smile, Greg's smile, and his blue eyes crinkled with pleasure. Striding across the drive, the gravel crunching under his old gardening shoes he stripped off his gardening gloves and held out his hand in welcome.

'My dear Zoe, this is a lovely surprise. I am pleased to see you.'

'I do hope you don't mind me coming over unasked, I hope you're not busy, only I wanted . . . '

He cut short her explanations.

'My dear girl, you are welcome at any

time. Of course I'm not busy. At least, I have nothing to do that can't wait and I'm always pleased for an excuse to knock off early. Do you like French beans?'

'Love them,' said Zoe.

'Give you some to take home. Just picked these from the garden. Come on, let's go and sit on the terrace and we can have a talk.' He led the way back round the house and settled Zoe on to the swing seat, then pulling up another chair for himself, he said, 'Now then, to business. You haven't come to tell me you've changed your mind about the job, I hope.'

Zoe laughed. 'No, the opposite in fact. I've come to ask you when I can start.'

Mr. Enodoc glanced curiously at her.

'There's no immediate hurry, is there? Not short of cash are you?'

Zoe might have resented such a comment from most people, but Mr. Enodoc spoke so ingenuously that it robbed the question of all offence.

She shook her head.

'No, I've no immediate problems there, I'm still being paid by Amalgamated Chemicals, it's just . . . ' and encouraged by his easy interest she told him briefly about Robert and Rosemary. She was surprised she had told him, and yet she felt as if she had known him a long time; perhaps it was because he was so like Gregory, or Gregory so like him that she could be at ease in the company of either.

Mr. Enodoc listened without comment until she had finished and then without Zoe having to explain that she needed to throw herself into hard work, to keep her mind occupied, he said, 'I think we should make a start on Monday morning, don't you? We'll work from half past nine till half past five. You can either have lunch here with me or, if you want a change of scene, the pub in the village does very good bar snacks. As for salary, how about . . . ' and he named a monthly salary that made Zoe's eyes stretch.

'Is that all all right?' he asked anxiously when still dazed Zoe had made no reply.

'Yes, that sounds marvellous,' she smiled across at him. 'I'm really looking forward to it.'

'Now then,' said Mr. Enodoc, 'Mrs. Mitchell is out this afternoon so I've got to fend for myself. Would you like a cup of tea?'

'I'd love one,' said Zoe. 'Shall I make it?'

'Let's go and see what she's left us. Usually some cakes and things.

'We'll have it outside,' said Mr. Enodoc when they had discovered a plate of sandwiches and some cake and biscuits under a clean white cloth on the kitchen table. They made a pot of tea and he carried it all out to the table on the terrace. When they had finished eating and were both sitting nursing a third cup of tea, Mr. Enodoc said, 'I gather you're back in your cottage now. How are you settling in? Any problems?'

Again without really meaning to, Zoe found herself telling Mr. Enodoc all about bricking up the cellar and then about the prowler who had disturbed her the night before. Again, being a good listener, he heard her out without comment or question until she said, 'I don't expect he'll come back again, but I'll be happier when the phone goes in. I meant to apply for one today, but with one thing and another I didn't. Never mind you can be sure I will tomorrow.'

'Yes,' agreed Mr. Enodoc, 'I think you should. These Penrose people are right when they say you're too isolated to be without one. Why didn't your aunt have one?'

'I don't know,' said Zoe. 'I expect she never had and it didn't worry her. I never knew her of course, so I don't know what sort of person she was. Perhaps she was anti 'new-fangled devices'!'

Mr. Enodoc grinned. 'Perhaps she was. I am myself a bit.'

Zoe drove back to Port Marsden

through a golden summer evening. The villages she passed basked in heavy sunlight, cottage gardens ablaze with July colours. She was tempted to stop at one of the village inns for a quiet drink in the garden and a basket of chicken and chips, but she was determined to be home well before the sun slipped below the horizon and dusk stole across the cliff to wreathe the cottage in shifting shadows. The doors would be shut and bolted and the curtains drawn across before she would switch on a light tonight, and indeed, the moment she got home she checked that every window and door was latched even though the sun had not yet set.

However, as the twilight deepened she heard the sound of a car and Barney barked, a warning or a welcome? Peeping out from behind a curtain Zoe saw the red MGB bumping along the track and pulling up behind the Mini. She suddenly realised how close her fear had been to the surface as she opened the door to let Greg inside.

He paused on the threshold and putting both hands on her shoulders held her at arm's length.

'Are you all right?' he demanded and there was suppressed anger in his voice. Zoe was surprised by both his tone and his action which had not been gentle.

'Of course I'm all right,' she replied defensively. 'Why shouldn't I be?'

'Why didn't you tell me? Why did I hear from other people?'

'Hear what?' Zoe pulled away from him.

'That you had an intruder last night. You should have come to me.'

Zoe turned and went into the sitting room and Greg followed her.

'Why didn't you come to me this morning, Zoe?' Greg asked a little more gently this time. Zoe looked across at him and her moment of anger faded as she saw the genuine concern in his eyes. She smiled and said, 'I went to the police and reported it. There was nothing you could do. How did you hear anyway?'

'My father's just been on the phone. I was out earlier, he's only just got through.'

'It's very good of you to come up, but there's nothing you can do really. Constable Dewar says they'll send a patrol car past from time to time, so I shan't be entirely cut off.'

Even though she spoke with courage Greg could hear the underlying fear in her voice and Zoe knew it so she continued with false brightness.

'Let's have a drink now you're here, or would you prefer coffee?' She slipped past him to the kitchen but he caught her arm and stayed her.

'Zoe,' he said softly 'Zoe, don't stay here alone tonight. If you must stay let me stay, too, I'll sleep down here and then,' his voice hardened, 'if that bastard does come back he'll have me to reckon with.' She raised her eyes to his and found them intently upon her as he repeated, 'Please let me stay.'

Zoe shook her head and tried to pull away again. She longed to feel Greg's arms about her, holding her close, holding her safe; she wanted him to kiss her, to feel the strength of his body against hers, but she knew that this was only because she was afraid and needed comfort, not because she felt deeply about him, and knowing intuitively that his feelings for her were strengthening every day, she was determined not to encourage him to feel what she could not return. But Gregory did not release her, instead he tightened his grip and twisted her round into his arms. For a moment he held her, his cheek against her hair as he said huskily, 'Oh, my darling Zoe, sweetheart, I couldn't bear it if anything happened to you.' Then lifting her face with his fingers he kissed her on her mouth, gently at first but then his lips more demanding as he felt the response in her; felt her arms tighten round his neck and her lips part beneath his for a moment before, suddenly, stiffening, she struggled to be free. Reluctantly he let her go and she moved from him, leaning weakly on the back of a chair.

'You'd better go now, Greg,' she said shakily. 'I shall be quite all right alone here.'

Greg took a step towards her saying, 'Come on now, Zoe, be sensible. I promise I won't touch you again. I won't come near you. I'm sorry, I'm a fool, it was all too soon, but let me at least stay . . . '

Zoe cut him short; angry because she had given in to her need for comfort, she snapped out, 'I'm quite all right, Gregory. Go. Go now. I don't want you to touch me, I don't want you here. Leave me alone.'

'Thank you for putting it so plainly,' said Gregory stiffly. 'You need not worry, I shan't trouble you again.' He left then, his face cold, his blue eyes expressionless.

Zoe spent a third sleepless night, but this time her tossing and turning had little to do with fear of an intruder.

She remembered the hurt look on Greg's face before the icy mask replaced it and she kept saying to herself, I was right. Right not to encourage him. I couldn't bear to hurt someone as Robert hurt me. Had Robert encouraged her to give him her heart? Sometimes he had kissed her but these occasions had been few and far between and the kisses had been brief and passionless. When he had however, her heart had wings for days afterwards. How terrible if Greg should come to love her when she felt only friendship for him.

I was right. I know I was right, she told herself determinedly but was still strangely unconvinced by all her logical arguments when at last she drifted off into an uneasy sleep. Indeed, as she finally sank into oblivion, it was with the taste of Gregory's kisses somehow still tingling on her lips.

In the morning still feeling tired and generally apathetic, Zoe made herself make the effort to go down to the vicarage as she had promised Mrs. Penrose, to offer her help for the church fête. Anne was pleased to see her and whisked her into the kitchen for a cup of coffee and a chat.

'You look tired,' remarked Anne as she handed Zoe a mug and perched on the edge of the kitchen table with her own.

'Sort of grey under the eyes.'

'Thanks very much,' said Zoe with a rueful grin, 'that's calculated to cheer me up.'

'Problems?' asked Anne and settled back to listen. Not wanting anyone else worrying about her living alone up on the cliff top Zoe did not mention the prowler who had so frightened her two nights earlier, but confided her encounter with Gregory.

'It's my own fault in a way,' she explained. 'I mean he's been such a good friend perhaps he thought I considered him more, and I'm determined not to lead him on in that direction.'

'And rightly if that's how you feel,' agreed Anne. 'But he knows about Robert, doesn't he, so he can't imagine you'll change overnight.'

'But he looked so hurt and then so angry, cold and angry.'

Anne laughed. 'Well,' she said 'I don't suppose he's been in this situation before. He's not used to it and doesn't like it. Usually it's the other way round, he's the one who's able to pick and choose his girlfriends. Almost all the girls in the neighbourhood have cast their eyes in his direction at some time or other, and he's remained comfortably unattached. A real heartbreaker, handsome, charming and uninvolved.'

'I certainly wasn't charming last night,' said Zoe. 'I told him to go away and leave me alone. I don't want to be involved either.' She sighed. 'I wish he hadn't been so angry. He seemed to take it very hard.'

'Don't worry' said Anne. 'It's probably only his pride that's hurt. He's noted for his sudden flashes of temper.

It never lasts long, he'll be back.'

'But I don't want him back' said Zoe fiercely. 'At least,' she added lamely, 'not on those terms.'

'How do you want him?' enquired Anne with interest.

'Just as a friend, that's all.' And Zoe, anxious now to change the subject, indeed wishing she had never broached it, went on, 'I'm going to get a telephone put in, but I'm not sure how to go about it. I must call at the post office on my way home.'

'No need to do that,' said Anne. 'I think you can get things in motion by ringing up a special number and asking. You can do that from here.'

'Can I?' said Zoe. 'That's great, I will if you don't mind. Where do I get the number to ring?'

'In the front of the telephone book, I think,' said Anne. 'We'll have a look in a minute. Finish your coffee first.'

'What I really came about,' said Zoe, 'was the church fête. Mrs. Penrose was trying to press me into service yesterday and to get away from her I said I'd come and talk to you about what I could do to help.'

'You don't have to do anything,' replied Anne.

'Oh, I'd like to,' said Zoe. 'It's just I'd rather give you a hand than get involved with Mrs. Penrose's end of things.'

Anne laughed at this and said, 'I can understand that, she can be a bit much at times. She means well though and when she's in charge, things do tend to get done. Don't worry, we'll fix you up helping with a stall or sideshow on the day and if anything comes up in the meantime I'll let you know. It's not till September and we're relatively well organised.'

Zoe felt better when she left the vicarage. Things had slipped back into perspective a little after her chat with Anne and she felt able to cope on her own again. Before she left she had rung the telephone sales department and applied for her phone and though she was told there might be some delay she felt she had done what she could and was happier.

After lunch Graham Spring turned up at Shearwater Cottage, a small trailer behind his car, laden with bricks, cement and tools.

'Don't you worry about me down there,' he told Zoe, 'I'll just get on with the job and let you know when its finished.'

'I'll be having a cup of tea later,' said Zoe. 'Shall I bring you a cup down?'

'No, thanks, I've a flask with me.'

'Well, if you're sure,' said Zoe, a guilty relief spreading through her because she would not have to go into the cellar before the hole was closed. 'I'll be up here if you want me.' But Mr. Spring did not call her until sometime later, when he stuck his head round the cellar door.

'I'm finished, Miss Carson. Would you like to come down and see?'

Zoe followed him down the steps and looked across to where the old door stood closed. Mr. Spring flung it open and there was a neat brick wall from ceiling to floor. The secret room had gone, and Zoe felt as if someone had removed an enormous weight from her shoulders. She smiled across at the builder.

'That's marvellous,' she said with feeling. 'I didn't really know how much that room was preying on my mind until you blocked it off.' She crossed over and closed the door and then said 'Do you know what would make it even better? Putting Queen Anne back in front so I can't even see the door.'

'Queen Anne?'

'That huge bookcase. We could move it together.'

'I remember moving this before in old Miss Carson's time. My mate and I had to shift it up the other end so she could have her logs near the steps. Heavy, that is, but we'll have a go.'

Together they eased the great book-case across the doorway so that the cellar looked as it had done the first time Zoe had entered it.

The builder collected his tools and drove away, and Zoe went back into the house to lock the cellar door and see about supper, her heart lighter than it had been for some time.

15

Monday morning dawned damp and wet, but the weather did not dampen Zoe's high spirits as she set out for Charfield Manor to start work on the library. She found she was really looking forward to having a regular job again, even after so short a break, particularly something that promised to be so interesting. Mr. Enodoc greeted her at the door and led her through into the library where the crates she had seen before still waited to be unpacked.

'Now,' said Mr. Enodoc, 'as far as I know these were packed in no particular order, so we're really starting from scratch. I shan't be with you much today so I'll explain what I want you to do and then leave you to get on. The first job will be to unpack these.' He went on to show her several card indexes each with different coloured cards for cross referencing each non-fiction book according to subject matter, title and author and two more indexes for the works of fiction that she found.

'When we've done all the books I bought from Rusham Grange, we'll do my own library which has never been catalogued either. If we do it in the same way we'll see at once as we file the cards if there are any duplicates. There are sure to be dozens and we can select the better one in each case to keep here and I'll sell the rest sometime when we've finished.'

As he talked Zoe began to realise the mammoth proportions of the job she had taken on, but she was pleased to be doing it and as soon as Mr. Enodoc left her she got to work. The morning flew by and when Mrs. Mitchell called her for lunch Zoe could hardly believe how the time had passed. She had drunk a cup of coffee mid-morning without pausing in her work and yet when lunch time came she had seemed scarcely to have begun.

Mr. Enodoc left her very much on her own that first week and Zoe was grateful. She soon slipped into her new routine and drew comfort from its regular pattern. She drove over to Charfield each morning and worked through until lunch, which she usually took with Mr. Enodoc. He was always a charming companion, extremely well-read and well-informed so that her lunch break was as interesting as her work. Then she would return to the books and work on. Often Mr. Enodoc would get Mrs. Mitchell to bring in a tea tray and he would join Zoe for the final hour to discuss the work and its progress.

When it was fine Zoe worked with the long windows thrown wide to the garden, the drifting fragrance of the honeysuckle and the murmur of its attendant bees reminding her it was summer outside; on wet days when rain curtained the garden and the windows were closed, she felt secure and warm surrounded by her hundreds of books. She grew to love these books, many with soft leather covers, some beautifully tooled. It was a pleasure to handle them, turning them over in her fingers, sniffing their indefinable odour of age. There were several first editions, some of which were obviously unread, their pages still uncut, and so she decided to start a first editions index as well which, when she showed it to Mr. Enodoc later that afternoon, pleased him greatly.

'I knew you'd make a good job of this,' he said delightedly. 'I couldn't have found anyone better.' And Zoe, flushed with pleasure at his compliment showed him the volumes of particular interest she had laid aside for him to see.

However, in all their conversations over lunch or in the library they very seldom mentioned Gregory. Zoe decided, having waited for the references to him which never came, that Greg must have warned his father of their quarrel, no, not quarrel exactly, disagreement, and he was tactfully steering clear of what might be an embarrassing or awkward topic; or maybe Mr. Enodoc was waiting for Zoe to mention Greg first. Either way Zoe was glad that his name did not crop up for she did not want to be drawn on that subject.

The days slipped into weeks and Zoe spent her weekends exploring the countryside around her new home. One Sunday after church she joined Anne and David for lunch and on another occasion Mrs. Penrose and James invited her to dinner and unable to think of a reasonable excuse, she accepted. Gregory did not come near her, indeed she did not even see him in the distance for which she was half sorry half glad; it saved any awkwardness between them after their last encounter, but she found she missed his cheerful company far more than she had expected.

As the day of the Church's Michaelmas fête drew nearer Anne found her several jobs to do, painting boards and wrapping parcels for the bran tub.

'On the day we wondered if you would take charge of knocking the guy's hat off,' said Anne. 'We have a guy propped up in a chair and they throw balls at his hat. Money back if you knock off his hat.'

'Yes, of course,' agreed Zoe. 'Who makes the guy? Not me, I hope!'

'No, no,' laughed Anne, 'the Sunday school children have made him. All you have to do is take the customer's money and see they keep their feet behind the line.'

The day before the fête Zoe had just got home from Charfield Manor when she heard a car approaching along the track. Before she looked out she thought she recognised the engine note and sure enough the MGB pulled up behind the Mini and Gregory clambered out.

Zoe felt a sudden warm pleasure at seeing him and opening the front door went out to greet him. He met her with a polite smile on his face which spread to a broad grin as he saw Zoe's welcoming smile.

'Hallo,' he said, and Zoe realised how much she had missed him. She took him indoors for a drink and ended up cooking omelettes for both of them.

'Don't you want to know why I came up?' asked Greg as they lingered over their coffee.

'If you want to tell me. Yes, of course I do.'

'I've had another offer for your cottage.'

'Another offer? But it's off the market.'

'Yes, I know, but apparently whoever received the details hasn't bothered to follow them up until now.'

'Very slow off the mark,' observed Zoe, 'who is it?'

'That's the thing I don't know, it's someone working through an agent again. Different one this time; anyway, when I said the cottage was no longer for sale the man said his client was prepared to offer considerably more than the asking price because he'd been looking for so long and Shearwater Cottage exactly suited his needs. I said I'd pass the message on and contact him again if you were interested in proceeding.'

'Well, I'm not,' said Zoe firmly. 'I'm settled in here and I'm quite happy so you can tell your agent his client will have to go on looking.'

'Fine, I'll tell him,' said Greg, closing the subject. 'Shall we go out for the day tomorrow? We could find a quiet pub for lunch or perhaps go into Truro.'

'Oh, Greg I'd have loved to,' said Zoe regretfully, 'but it's the Church fête and I'm running one of the side shows. I can't let them down now.'

'No, of course not,' agreed Greg. 'What about dinner in the evening then? You'll need resuscitation by the time the fête's over.'

'I'm afraid I can't even do that,' said Zoe. 'All the helpers are invited to a fork supper at Shearwater House in the evening; I've already accepted the invitation.'

'Then next weekend?' suggested Greg. 'Unless you'd rather not.'

'I'd like that,' said Zoe simply. 'I'm not making excuses for tomorrow, Greg, I'm already committed, that's all.'

Greg smiled. 'Yes, I know. I'll phone you at Charfield during the week to arrange it with you. Your phone's not in here yet, is it?'

'No, it isn't,' said Zoe. 'I must chase that up. I'd forgotten about it actually.' Strangely that was true, for having settled comfortably into Shearwater Cottage and with no further trouble with prowlers or peeping Toms, Zoe had hardly noticed her lack of telephone.

'I should ask again' said Greg, 'chivvy them a bit. In the meantime I'll phone you at Charfield.'

When he left, Greg made no move to touch Zoe, he simply walked out to his car, waved briefly and roared away into the darkness.

Next day was grey and overcast and when Zoe joined the band of helpers setting up the stalls and sideshows on the lawns of Shearwater House she was greeted by an almost distraught Mrs. Penrose.

'It's going to pour, my dear, I know it's going to pour. We shall have to move indoors, I've cleared the billiard room, but we'll never get everyone in. I don't know what we shall do.'

David Campion tried to soothe her a little, saying that the forecast was good and it should be sunny by lunchtime. While he was calming Mrs. Penrose, Zoe made good her escape and went to find Anne. It did not take them long to set up Zoe's sideshow; it was merely a question of propping up the beautiful guy the Sunday school had made and setting his bowler hat on his huge papier-maché head and marking out the throwing lines. Behind the chair they rigged a blanket screen for the balls to hit when they missed the hat and all was ready for the paying public to arrive. Zoe then helped with the laying out of other stalls.

It was chaotic with people rushing about carrying ladders, trestle tables, bunting and chairs. David stood, the calm eye of the storm, giving advice and instructions while everyone gyrated around him. Mrs. Penrose dashed about doing very little other than getting in the way and James was nowhere to be seen.

David was right and by the time Zoe had returned from snatching an hour's respite and a bite of lunch at home the sky had cleared and the September sun was beaming on the whole proceedings. At two-thirty sharp the wife of the local M.P., resplendent in a huge floral hat, declared the fête open and then made a tour of every stall and sideshow admiring everything, gracious as royalty on a walkabout. She tried her hand at several of the games and pausing at Zoe's she said, indicating the guy, 'What a beautifully horrible chap he is, I shouldn't want to bump into him on a dark night. Did you make him your-self?' Zoe laughed and shook her head. 'No,' she replied, 'the Sunday school children did.'

'Did they indeed?' remarked the M.P.'s wife. 'Sunday school was far less exciting in my day. What am I supposed to do?'

'Knock his hat off.'

She paid her money, tried and failed, and then moved on, saying to David who was still with her, 'You should keep him for Bonfire Night, those children have gone to a lot of trouble, haven't they?'

'That's a good idea,' agreed David and turning back to Zoe called out, 'when it's all over, Zoe, put the dummy into my car, I'll look after him until November the fifth,' and Zoe, busy with a rush of customers, waved her hand in acknowledgement.

The afternoon proved a great suc-cess. Zoe kept an eye open for Gregory in case he had decided to give the fête his support, but she knew it was not the sort of event which would interest him and was not surprised when he did not appear. By six o'clock the public had departed. The children's fancy dress had been paraded and judged, the final of bowling for the pig had been decided, most of the stalls had been denuded, the raffle had been drawn and innumerable cups of tea had been drunk.

The lawns of Shearwater House looked like the scene of a hurricane, but nobody cared and gradually order was restored as each stallholder totted up the afternoon's take, handed it in to David now installed in the Shearwater House morning room and began to dismantle stalls, tents and awnings. By half past seven the lawns were clear and everyone assembled in the dusk on the terrace where James was dispensing well earned glasses of beer or wine.

Zoe hadn't been long in taking down the screen and moving the guy from his chair to the back seat of David's car.

I'd better warn Anne he's there, she

thought as she saw the ugly painted face leering at her from the back window. She'll get the fright of her life if she catches sight of him unexpectedly, and shaking her satisfactorily heavy tin of money she went to the morning room to hand it in before going on in search of Anne; then not long after she was perched on the terrace wall sipping cool white wine, glad to take the weight off her feet and happy to be surrounded by laughing friendly people.

'There's nothing like a do like this for breaking the ice and getting to know people,' said Anne as she introduced Zoe around the group.

The evening shadows lengthened across the lawn and once the sun had gone a chill in the air reminded them that autumn had arrived. Shepherded by Mrs. Penrose they all proceeded indoors to the buffet laid out in the dining room. The food was superb: an enormous selection of cold meats, salads and sauces; baked potatoes smothered in melting butter, warm crisp garlic bread and a sweet trolley that groaned under its load of gateaux, trifles, meringues and fruit salad. Mrs. Penrose had excelled herself and Zoe congratulated her warmly.

'It's the most marvellous spread I've ever seen,' she said.

'My dear Zoe, how kind of you to say so! Do help yourself to more. James, help Zoe to some more turkey.'

'Oh no, I really couldn't,' protested Zoe, laughing as James came across.

'Then have some more wine,' he insisted and refilled Zoe's glass.

Suddenly the warm room, the smoke from the cigarettes and fatigue from a busy day all reacted on Zoe and she decided to go home. She had walked over after lunch, because as James pointed out, 'The nearest parking place'll probably be your own drive anyway.'

Not wanting to draw attention to her departure because she was afraid James would insist on seeing her home, Zoe slipped out on to the terrace and from there circled the house to the rhododendron walk. It was full darkness now and there was only a quarter moon to light her way, but as her eyes grew accustomed to the night she was able to follow the driveway well enough and emerging on to the road found the entrance to her own track across the cliff top to the cottage. As she followed this through the darkness she could not help but recall the intruder of several weeks earlier. She looked round her a little fearfully and a rustle in the hedgerow made her start and catch her breath. Anxious to be safely inside her house Zoe quickened her step, her feet crunched on the stones and she stopped abruptly. Silence closed in round her and she made herself walk on.

Ahead was the stubby silhouettc of the cottage crouching against the night sky. There were no lights on because leaving the place at midday she had not thought to leave any. Now she wished she had. The moonlight was faint, but enough to guide her to her front door without mishap. From inside the house Barney barked and Zoe called out, 'Quiet Barney, it's only me.' Scrabbling in the depths of her handbag she found her key and with it poised ready for the keyhole she stepped into the porch. Her scream made Barney start to bark again and she shrank back from the house, sobbing with fear. Swinging gently in the wind faintly visible now she knew it was there, was a body dangling from the porch beam. She stared at it in horror, as it twisted gently round first one way and then back again. For a moment panic rooted her to the spot, but Barney's incessant barking brought her to her senses again and she fought to control her terror.

If only Greg was here, she thought and moved instinctively towards her car, her link with the rest of the world. She edged towards it in the darkness and suddenly losing her nerve dashed to it, wrestling with the door in her haste to get inside. She switched on the headlamps and the strong white beams pierced the blackness lighting up the porch and its gruesome occupant. The body was still twisting on its rope and as she turned round the headlights picked out the face, the ugly painted face of the church fête dummy. With a noose round its neck the body hung awkwardly, the face at a hideous angle, but Zoe's relief made her shake and as she realised this must be some childish prank merely to frighten her, her fear turned to anger.

Leaving the headlights to illuminate the front of the cottage she strode up to the porch and pushing past the dangling dummy opened the front door and switched on all the lights downstairs. Then she drew all the curtains in case the perpetrator of the prank was lurking nearby to enjoy her discovery of the dummy. She took a sharp, kitchen knife and cut the rope, tossing the body on to the garden, then having been back to the car to douse the lights and lock the doors, she returned to the cottage and closed and locked the front door before her legs finally gave out and she sunk shaking on to the stairs while Barney anxiously licked her face.

16

Zoe decided to take the dummy over to the vicarage after church the next day but when she came out of the cottage on the Sunday morning the guy had gone. The rope was still made fast to the porch beam but there was no sign of the body it had suspended. Zoe shuddered to think that someone had been able to approach the house that closely without alerting Barney.

Perhaps the joker had indeed been watching and as soon as she had closed the door had retrieved the guy and perhaps even returned it to Shearwater House.

She decided not to mention the incident to anyone but put it behind her and ignore it. After all, there was no point in the prank and in the cheerful sunlight she was inclined to view it as a childish joke. So she said nothing to anyone until the next day when at lunchtime Mr. Enodoc asked if the telephone had been installed yet. Zoe replied that it had not, and added, 'But I could have done with it last night. Somebody played a horrible practical joke on me.'

When he heard what had happened Mr. Enodoc said, 'I can see no harm was done, but it was clearly a frightening experience. I don't like the idea of you stuck out there without a phone. I think I might be able to move things along a bit if you'd like me to; friends in high places, you know.' He grinned and Zoe said, 'I would be very grateful if you could.'

Before she left Charfield Manor that evening Mr. Enodoc popped his head into the library and said cheerfully, 'You should be linked up to a phone before the end of the week. Don't forget to let me know the number.'

He was quite right. How he had organised it for her Zoe did not know, but by the end of the week the phone was in and she felt less cut off. The friends to whom she gave the number were all relieved to know she was no longer so isolated.

Her pleasure at the telephone's installation was short-lived. She had only had it a week or so when the first unpleasant call came. She was cooking supper and the phone rang; at first when she answered it there was just heavy breathing and then a horrific laugh. She slammed down the receiver and stood for a moment, her heart pounding.

The calls continued, sometimes several in one evening, sometimes only once every three or four days. Zoe came to dread the telephone's jangling, never knowing if she would find Greg or Anne or Mrs. Penrose on the line, or if it would be the man. It was after he actually spoke to her for the first time that Zoe took action. The phone had rung soon after she got home from work and Zoe almost did not answer it, but it seemed so insistent, and she did not want the caller, whoever it might be to think the cottage empty, so at last she picked up the receiver. The man began to speak at once, as if from a prepared statement.

'I thought I might come up and see you tonight,' he drawled. 'I came once before but you wouldn't let me in. There are so many things I'd like to do to you. We'd be all alone and I'd so enjoy your company.'

Zoe listened, terrified and yet somehow unable to hang up.

'Why?' she whispered. 'Why me? Leave me alone.'

'Alone!' The voice picked up the word. 'Yes, I'd love to get you alone. Last time you shut the curtains in my face. If you did that again I'd probably break the window and come in to teach you not to be so naughty.'

'Go away,' shrieked Zoe, 'go away. I'm calling the police.'

She slammed down the receiver and looked round her in terror. All the windows were still open to freshen the

258

house which had been shut up all day and in an explosion of panic she rushed round the cottage slamming and bolting the outside doors and closing the windows. Although it was not dark she was tempted to draw all the curtains but terrified of the caller's final threat she decided she would leave them open while she called the police at least. She dialled the police house and P.C. Dewar said he would come up at once. Then she phoned Greg, but there was was no reply. She tried the vicarage but the line was engaged. She made no effort to phone the Penroses. Mrs. Penrose wailing, 'I told you so' did not suit Zoe's mood.

P.C. Dewar arrived within minutes and when Zoe saw the car drive up she felt the tension within her snap and tears streamed down her face. She unbolted the door and let him in and with one look at her he took her into the sitting room, sat her down and waited patiently for her to collect herself again.

'I'm awfully sorry,' she said after a while 'I didn't mean to do that.'

'Don't worry, Miss Carson, it probably did you good. Now then, how about making a pot of tea and telling me exactly what's been going on.'

Zoe did so and when he had heard her out he said, 'It must have been very frightening, but this kind of call is, unfortunately, common enough. Some men get their kicks this way, and once they've found a number that's answered by a woman each time, they keep calling it. They very seldom carry out their threats, you know.'

'But he's already been up here,' said Zoe, fear creeping back into her voice.

'He says he has. May not be the same chap as your prowler.'

'But he knew I pulled the curtains in his face.'

'True,' agreed P.C. Dewar. 'It is, of course, quite possible he is the same one.'

'But it's a new phone,' pointed out Zoe. 'I'm not in a directory yet.'

'No, but you're not ex-directory are you?'

'No, I haven't asked to be.'

'Then your number will be obtainable through directory enquiries, the new numbers list. If it is the peeping Tom he could find it that way.'

'What am I going to do?' cried Zoe.

'Well, we'll give it a day or so and if he calls again we'll get an intercept put on the phone. Then you must keep him talking while we trace the call. But he may not call again.'

P.C. Dewar continued to be reassuring while he drank his cup of tea and then suddenly the phone rang. Zoe froze, her face ashen, but P.C. Dewar crossed to the phone and picked up the receiver.

'Hallo,' he said.

'Hallo,' said a man's voice. 'Who's that?'

'This is Police Constable Dewar, more to the point, who is that?'

'Gregory Enodoc. Where's Miss Carson?'

'She's here, hang on a minute.'

Constable Dewar put his hand over the mouthpiece and said 'Mr. Gregory Enodoc.' Zoe took the phone and Greg on hearing why the police were at Shearwater Cottage said briefly, 'I'm on my way over. I'm at Charfield but I'll be there as quickly as I can.'

Constable Dewar left and Zoe spent an anxious half hour waiting for Greg to arrive. P.C. Dewar had drawn the curtains in the living room and she sat in there with Barney by her side until she heard Greg arrive. She recognised the roar of the car, but she did not open the door until she heard his voice and was positive it was he.

'Are you all right?' he demanded as he closed the front door behind him and shot the bolt.

'Yes, just a bit frightened, but I'll get over that, as long as he doesn't ring again.'

'Well, he may do,' said Greg bluntly. 'Don't listen to him, just put the phone down.'

'That's easier said than done,' retorted

Zoe and immediately Greg was contrite.

'I didn't mean you'd been encouraging him, but people like that get tired of the game when their victims don't react.'

'What do you know about people like that?' asked Zoe sharply.

'No more than anyone else,' said Greg calmly.

Zoe sighed. 'I'm sorry, I didn't mean to snap. I'm still a bit tense, that's all.'

'I know, don't worry. Come on let's have a drink to cheer ourselves up. What have you got hidden away?'

'Medicinal brandy.'

'Medicinal brandy it is. What could be more appropriate!'

He found the bottle and a couple of glasses in the cupboard and poured two generous measures then sat down and looked across at Zoe.

'Now,' he said, 'let's talk about something else. Did you know there was a harbour cottage coming up for sale on the square?'

Zoe shook her head and sipping her brandy, she said, 'Tell me about it.'

'It's one of the row beside the harbour. It has the same accommodation as this and a view out across the sea.' He looked at her across the top of his glass.

'If you sold this place and bought that you would have a lovely cottage, but you would not be so isolated as you are up here. You'd have neighbours; people within call if you needed help. You'd be a much more difficult target for an intruder because the square is well lit.'

'I don't want to move. I love this place despite the difficulties. Now that the cellar is safe I'm not afraid to be in it alone.'

'Unless you have nuisance phone calls.'

'I could get those anywhere.'

'Agreed, but whoever it is knows you're by yourself here. Of course it's up to you, but do think about that harbour cottage. I could accept that good offer we had on this one, or find another buyer.'

'I'll think about it. By the way Constable Dewar said not to mention the calls to anyone, except you of course. He thinks it must be someone local, who knows the lie of the land and if they do have to put an intercept on the line he doesn't want it to get around.'

'Don't worry, I shan't say a word. Where shall we go on Saturday?'

The previous Saturday they had driven up on to Bodmin moor, lunched in a little village pub, then directed by the landlord, had spent the afternoon exploring the countryside around. Zoe had thoroughly enjoyed the day. She was pleased to be out in the fresh air after her days in Charfield Manor library and as they sat by a stream watching little brown trout darting in the chuckling water and the autumn sun streamed down and struck hot on her shoulders, she felt completely at ease with the tall man stretched out beside her, and was glad that in spite of the night in the cottage when he had held her in his arms and called her sweetheart and her rejection of him, they could still be friends; each comfortable in the company of the other. Greg rolled over and tossed a handful of pebbles into the stream.

'We must do this again some time,' he had said idly. And Zoe replied, 'Yes, we must.'

'Next Saturday?'

'If you like.'

And each evening after that Greg had phoned. He had asked her out for a drink, but Zoe, remembering her determination not to let Gregory come too close, for his own good, refused, but softened her refusal by saying she was looking forward to Saturday.

She was glad he was here now though, for the telephone call had frightened her more than she cared to admit. She looked across at his face now so familiar with its square cut jaw and determined chin, firm mouth and the etched laughter lines around his blue blue eyes, and was reassured by his inherent strength. He looked up for her answer to his question, 'Where shall we go on Saturday?' and saw her scrutiny. For a moment he returned her look with seriousness and then he grinned and said, 'Well?'

Zoe, unaware that her study of him had been observed as she brought herself back to answer said, 'It depends on the weather really, don't you think? You surprise me.'

'Mystery tour?'

'Why not?'

As Greg was leaving he said to Zoe, 'Why don't you leave the receiver off for the rest of the night? Then you'll know there'll be no more calls. No one important'll want to phone before morning, will they?'

'I shouldn't think so,' said Zoe. 'I think that's a good idea.' And when she had locked the door behind him she took the receiver off the hook before going up to bed.

Next morning, just before she left for Charfield and soon after she had replaced the receiver, the phone shrilled out. Zoe jerked the phone to her ear and said sharply, 'Hallo.'

'You naughty girl, you took the phone off, and I wanted to talk to you again. You had too many visitors for me to come and see you last night. Another time, perhaps. Tonight . . . ?'

Zoe slammed the receiver down and within seconds the telephone rang again. Answering it immediately, Zoe cried, 'Go away. I don't want to talk to you.'

'Zoe? Zoe? Is that you?' Zoe sank into a chair with relief. It was only Mrs. Penrose.

'Yes, Mrs. Penrose, I'm sorry I thought you were someone else.'

'Oh, I see. Well, I'm sorry to ring so early but I wanted to catch you before you went to work; the telephone was engaged last evening.'

'I'm sorry, I must have left it off the hook.'

'Well, anyway, dear, James is out for a while tonight and I get so lonely all by myself, I wondered if you'd come up and have supper with us and then perhaps spend the evening with me until James gets back.'

Zoe was about to make an excuse when it crossed her mind that she would not have to spend the evening alone waiting for the phone to ring if she went over to Shearwater House and so she replied, 'How nice, Mrs. Penrose. I'd love to come.'

'We'll expect you at about half past seven then. I won't keep you now. Good-bye, dear.'

From Charfield Manor Zoe rang Constable Dewar and told him that there had been another call that morning. He was immediately concerned and said he would see what could be done about tapping the phone in the hope of tracing the calls.

'But you must keep him on the phone for as long as possible,' and Zoe said she would try. She was tempted to tell Mr. Enodoc about the unpleasant calls, but decided that Constable Dewar was probably right and that the fewer people who knew of them the better.

As she was getting ready to go to the Penroses that evening the phone rang again. Remembering she had to keep the caller talking for as long as she could she took a deep breath and answered. It was Greg.

'Are you all right?' he asked. 'Any more calls?'

'One, I'll tell you all about it on Saturday.'

'Shall I come over this evening?'

'No, thanks. I'm going to supper at the Penroses'.'

Greg laughed. 'Are you indeed? Have fun.'

'I will,' said Zoe. 'Goodbye.'

There was one more call before she left the house and this time the now familiar slightly muffled yet lascivious voice said, 'Home again. Time to put your feet up and relax. Maybe I'll pop over and join you, we could relax together. Will you wear your bathrobe again for me? How I'd love to take it off. Peel you slowly like a beautiful orange.'

Trying not to listen to what he was actually saying Zoe kept thinking, Keep him talking, so when he paused she said a little shakily, 'Why do you keep phoning me? Why me? What do you want?' He went on as if he had not heard her question.

'What a lovely white body you have, I love smooth bodies, beautiful dark hair on smooth white shoulders. But I must fly now. I'll be seeing you, some time, sooner or later.' He laughed and the phone went dead. Zoe stood clutching the telephone wondering if he had been on the line for long enough. Then she carefully replaced the receiver and locked up the cottage, leaving on all the downstairs lights.

Mrs. Penrose welcomed Zoe as always, smothering her with warmth as she took her jacket and shepherded her into the lounge. James was there reading the paper and he got to his feet as Zoe came in. Soon she was installed in a chair with a sherry in her hand and Mrs. Penrose longing to hear about her work at Charfield Manor. Over supper round the dining room table, James said casually. 'There's a cottage up for sale in the village, you know.'

'Is there?' Zoe was non-committal.

'Yes, one of those by the harbour. If you sold Shearwater Cottage and bought that you wouldn't be so cut off as you are now.'

'Has Gregory been talking to you?'

'Gregory Enodoc?' James sounded surprised. 'No, I haven't seen him, why?'

'It's just that he suggested I move into the village as well.'

'It's because we worry about you, dear,' cried Mrs. Penrose. 'All alone. Supposing there was an accident, you might not get help for days.'

'I've the telephone,' said Zoe defensively.

'Indeed you have, but that's sometimes a mixed blessing.'

Zoe looked up sharply. 'What do you mean?' Had Mrs. Penrose heard about the calls?

'I mean, dear, that because you have the phone people assume you are all right, able to call for help in an emergency, but suppose you fell and broke your leg you might not be able to get to the phone and no one would know.'

'Oh, come on, Mother,' said James testily. 'That's a bit unlikely. All I wanted to do was to be sure Zoe knew she has the chance of moving down into the village if she wants to. That's all.'

Zoe thanked him and said she would bear it in mind.

After supper James excused himself saying he would be back in time to see Zoe home and left her to play Scrabble with Mrs. Penrose who was surprisingly good at the game and beat Zoe three times running. When James returned to walk her home she found she had really enjoyed her evening at Shearwater House. As she thanked Mrs. Penrose for her hospitality, the old lady said, 'I'm having a day in Plymouth on Saturday, shopping for some winter clothes. Would you care to come, too? The shops are very good there, they've some beautiful clothes.'

'That's a very kind thought' replied Zoe, 'but I'm afraid I'm already going out for the day on Saturday. Another time perhaps.'

'Of course,' cried Mrs. Penrose 'I'll be going again for Christmas shopping. Where are you off to? Somewhere nice?'

'I'm not sure. We're deciding on Saturday when we see what the weather's like. I'm going with Gregory.'

Mrs. Penrose's lips tightened but she said, 'How nice for you. Out to dinner, too, I suppose.'

'I expect so,' said Zoe. 'He said all day.'

She was glad to accept James's offer of an escort home for she did not want to approach the empty cottage alone in the dark. She was sure if the caller had crept across the cliff to the house he would leave again once he saw she was not by herself. Whether he was indeed lurking in the garden and ran off she did not know, but there were no further disturbances that night and with the receiver lying on the table beside the phone she passed a quiet night, sleeping deeply and woke feeling refreshed.

17

When Gregory arrived at Shearwater Cottage on Saturday morning the sky was a clear blue and the sun streamed down on to the cliff top. Patches of gorse shone, polished gold, and the dry spikey turf gleamed silver-green away to the cliff edge. The roof was off the MGB and the car, lovingly waxed and polished, reflected the sun's brilliance back to the sky.

Zoe, seeing the hood was down, put on her sheepskin coat, collected a scarf to cover her hair, and leaving Barney in the kitchen, locked the door and stepped out into the glorious October morning to begin Greg's mystery tour.

They drove out of Port Marsden as if taking the Charfield road, but then Greg turned off and meandered through narrow lanes until Zoe was completely lost. As before, they stopped for lunch at a village pub and then after an excellent lunch Greg drove them to Tremark Place. Zoe had never heard of it, but when she asked the landlord of the inn about it he had high praise.

'That's a beautiful place,' he said. 'Known for its gardens that is. You'll like them.'

He was right, Zoe was enchanted the moment she saw it; the mansion standing proud and tall against the sky and its gardens spread like a cloak about it.

'It's the gardens that are open to the public,' said Greg 'and they really are magnificent.' He parked the car and bought tickets at the gate which led into the grounds.

It was comparatively late in the season and the flood of high summer tourists had dwindled to a mere trickle. Almost alone in the gardens they wandered along shaded walks beneath trees dressed in their autumn gold, crimson and russet. The lawns, billiard-table smooth, stretched across behind the house to an ornamental lake where a pair of swans sailed, a fleet of half grown brown and white cygnets still behind them. Formal gardens were laid out beside the east wing of the house complete with a box hedge maze, and a walled garden with fruit trees on its sunbaked southern side, was sheltered by the west wing.

Entirely easy in the other's company, Zoe and Gregory explored it all, marvelling at the diversity of garden within one place, loving the peace and tranquillity of it all but at last coming to rest in a corner of the walled garden in the shade of a gnarled apple tree, still burdened with fruit.

So far that day Gregory had not asked about the telephone calls and kept their conversation to very general topics. Zoe, pleased to leave the ever present fear behind her for a day had taken the lead from him and had managed to spend several hours without hearing the terrifying voice echoing in her ears. Now, when she was completely relaxed he suddenly said, 'Are Robert and Rosemary married yet?' Zoe stared at him, angry at his probing a sensitive spot, and replied coldly, 'I haven't a clue. Let's talk about something else.'

'All right' said Greg easily. 'Had any good phone calls lately?'

'That's not funny, Gregory. Anyone would think they were a joke. Why bring them up now and ruin a lovely day?'

'Of course they aren't a joke,' answered Greg. 'But you need a safety valve. If I'm the only one who knows about these calls which you say I am, barring the police of course, then you must talk to me. Have there been any more?'

Zoe sighed. She knew Greg was right, in a way she did want to talk, as if to lance a boil to allow all the poison, the poison of fear to seep out and away.

'He's rung several times. The police have put a tap on the line, but though I try to talk to him he's never been on long enough to establish a trace. They've told me they need twice as long. It's as if he had a prepared speech each time and when he's made it he rings off.'

'Perhaps he knows the danger of talking too long, perhaps he's assumed the police are in on it now,' suggested Greg.

'I'm sure he knows,' said Zoe, 'and if he does we'll never catch him. The trouble is I'm afraid he may come to the cottage again, and I shall never be free of that fear until he's caught.'

'Or until you move out,' said Greg. 'Did you give any thought to the harbour cottage I mentioned?'

'That's a funny thing,' said Zoe, diverted for a moment, 'James Penrose mentioned that place, too. The Penroses were trying to persuade me to move as well.'

'Did he now,' pondered Greg with interest. 'I wonder how he came to hear of it. As far as I know it's not common knowledge yet.'

'Mrs. Penrose discovered it, I expect' said Zoe. 'She is a fountain of information as to what goes on in the town. I never knew anyone so ready to pass on the latest gossip.'

'It's probably a device to stop people talking about her; she makes everyone else seem more exciting. I've always thought there could be more to her than meets the eye.'

Zoe shrugged. 'Could be. Certainly she nearly always gets her own way.'

'And she thinks you should move to escape these calls.'

'Oh, she doesn't know about the calls, but she does think I'm too isolated there, that I shouldn't live there alone.'

'She could be right,' said Greg gently. 'I don't think you should either.'

'Well, I'm not going to be frightened out of my own home,' declared Zoe roundly. 'It is my home now and I don't intend to leave just because someone sets out to scare me away.'

'Is that what the caller is trying to do?'

'How do I know? It's not the only thing that's happened, is it?' And she reminded Greg about the guy hanging in the porch. He had, she knew, already heard the story from his father, but now he gave it more careful consideration.

'And you don't think it was just a prank any more?' he asked at last.

'I don't know what to think. It's been on my mind again lately.'

'Well, let's assume for a moment that you're right in your theory that someone is trying to scare you out of your cottage. The next question, is, why? Why does anyone want you out?'

Zoe shrugged again. 'I don't know,' she sighed. 'After all there's nothing there any more. I mean if this had happened before they discovered Jarvis in the cellar, I could have understood it.'

'Not at the time,' pointed out Greg. 'You didn't know he was there.'

'No,' agreed Zoe, 'but what I mean is, if the cellar room was still being used I could understand the need to get me out. I'd always be too close for comfort.'

'How do we know,' said Greg slowly, 'how do we know for sure that the cellar room isn't in use again?'

'What?' Zoe was incredulous. 'Come off it, Greg, it's all been bricked up. No one can get in.'

'Not from your side, I agree. Have you been down to the cellar since that bricklayer did the job?'

'No,' said Zoe. 'I haven't needed to.'

'Who recommended the man you used to do the job?'

'James did. He sent him round to look and then the next day he came back and did the job for me. He was remarkably efficient actually.'

'So no one could get into the cellar from your side?'

'Not without breaking down the brick wall, no.'

'But they could from elsewhere.'

'Elsewhere?'

'Where else do we know the tunnel comes out?'

'The cliff face . . . '

'Which is blocked. And?'

'James's cellar, which is now also blocked.'

'How do you know?'

'He told me.'

'Have you seen it all bricked off?' asked Greg.

'No, of course I haven't seen it,' replied Zoe, 'but he told me he was going to have it done.'

'Who has been trying to get you to move down to the village?'

'You have,' replied Zoe sharply.

'Agreed,' admitted Greg, 'but one of those passages from your cellar doesn't come up in mine.'

'You mean James?'

'I mean James. Think about it, sweetheart, he never did like you being there. Suppose it was he who was hiding Jarvis before getting him out of the country. You arriving really would have put a spanner in the works. They didn't know you were coming, did they?'

'Well, come to think of it they did ask me to let them know when I was coming down. To phone ahead so they could air the cottage for me.'

'And did you?'

'No, I didn't want to trouble them. It wasn't as if the place were damp.'

'There you are then,' said Greg triumphantly. 'They didn't know you were back in the cottage until they had their man trapped in the cellar below.'

'Now hold on, Greg,' protested Zoe, holding up her hand. 'Hold on. This is pure speculation.'

'It is and it isn't' said Greg. 'I've been doing some checking, using the old pal's act in a couple of places and I'm almost certain that the offers for your cottage came from James Penrose; indirectly, as I told you, but I think I've traced them both back to him.'

'James wants to buy the cottage?' Zoe was unbelieving. 'Then why didn't he say so while it was still on the market?'

'Probably wanted it at a knockdown price and waited. Then he heard you were staying permanently and he moved into action in two ways. Like coaxing a recalcitrant donkey, a little stick and a little carrot. Trying to encourage you to leave gently and trying to frighten you off when you stayed put.'

'I can't believe it,' said Zoe flatly. 'He and his mother have always been so kind to me.'

'Of course they have,' said Gregory soothingly, 'except of course when they're making obscene phone calls, leering in through windows and turning your front porch into a gibbet.'

'Don't!' cried Zoe shuddering. 'Listen, Greg,' she was imploring, 'this is all guesswork. We've no proof. James is in business in import and export, I've got his card somewhere.'

'Well,' said Greg unrelenting, 'he exports escaped convicts — in damaged condition, too. I wonder what he imports. What is the quality of the merchandise there? How long does he offer storage facilities?' Gregory's words rang a bell in Zoe's head. She clapped her hand to her forehead and said softly, 'Wait a minute, wait a minute. What was it she said, something about a problem with storage facilities.'

'Who?' demanded Greg. 'Who said that?'

'It was just something I overheard Mrs. Penrose say on the phone one day; something about not being able to accept any more merchandise at the moment as they no longer had storage facilities.'

'That's it then,' said Greg excitedly, jumping to his feet.

'It could be it.' Zoe was far from convinced. 'What do we do next?'

'We'll buy some food and I'll cook you dinner,' said Greg, 'at your place.'

'Oh, Gregory,' cried Zoe, exasperated, 'that's not what I meant.'

'Ulterior motive, sweetheart. I'd like to have a little look at that brick wall in your cellar.'

His mind would not be altered and so they hurried back through the quiet gardens to the car and just caught the shop in the nearest village before it closed for the weekend.

'I was going to take you out for a decent meal,' apologised Gregory. 'I've booked a table, but I'm afraid all they had in the shop were these.' And he tossed two tinned steak and kidney pies, a packet of frozen peas and a packet of frozen chips on to Zoe's lap.

'You don't mind too much do you?' he asked a little anxiously. 'I'll make it up to you, I promise.' Zoe looked at the forlorn pile of groceries on her knees and started to laugh, and having started, she laughed until she could laugh no more. Greg watched her his eyes alight with amusement and then said, 'Fine, that's settled then.'

When they reached Shearwater Cottage they were greeted by an ecstatic Barney who when he had greeted them rushed out into the garden barking. Greg followed him. 'Who's there, dog?' He paused outside the living room window. There were footprints in the flowerbed. He looked beneath the other downstairs windows. There were more footprints there. Someone had been peering in all round the house. A peeping Tom or someone checking the cottage was empty? Greg wondered. He went back to the kitchen but said nothing of his find to Zoe. He solemnly read the instructions on the tinned pies and put them into the oven.

'Now,' he said, 'a good half hour before I have to start the vegetables, let's have a look in that cellar.'

Zoe, unafraid now Gregory was with her, unlocked the cellar door and together they descended the steps. Greg switched on the light at the bottom and asked, surprised, 'Who put Queen Anne back?'

'I did,' said Zoe, 'with the builder. I asked him to help me. I didn't want her standing about in the middle of the floor.'

'Well, we'll have to shift her again,' said Greg. 'Come on.'

Yet again Zoe put her shoulder to the

great bookcase and together they inched it away from the wall until it was well clear. Behind it was the old door exactly as they had seen it the first time. Greg flung it open only to be confronted by a new red brick wall.

'There,' said Zoe, 'it hasn't been touched.'

'Just a minute, just a minute' said Greg impatiently, 'let's have a proper look at it.' He peered hard at the brickwork and then ran his fingers over it, testing edges and surfaces from top to bottom. Zoe watched, waiting for him to be satisfied. Then he suddenly said, 'Did you ask for airbricks to be put in?'

'Airbricks?'

'Yes, look here, along the top and along the bottom there is a layer of airbricks.'

'So?'

'So that means the little room beyond is as well ventilated as it ever was. See, there's a crack at the top and bottom of the door, where it doesn't fit exactly and these bricks are in the same places, so there must be a fair old draught through them.' He paused and took hold of Zoe by the shoulders. 'Can I take this wall down?'

Zoe was startled. 'Take the wall down?'

'Yes, I promise I'll have it replaced, but I've a feeling that if we knock it down we shall find evidence beyond of the room still being in use.'

'Shouldn't we tell the police then?' asked Zoe.

'Not until we're sure,' said Greg. 'If there's nothing I'll get it all bricked up again and no one will even know we looked. Have you got a chisel and a heavy hammer?'

'No,' said Zoe firmly, 'I haven't.'

'Never mind,' said Greg. 'I have. I'll go home and fetch one. You could cook the chips,' he added, 'and we'll eat before I start.'

While they were eating in companionable silence, the required hammer and chisel awaiting use on the side in the kitchen, Zoe tried to come to terms with the idea that James Penrose was responsible for the body in the cellar and for terrorizing her since its discovery.

'I don't understand it,' she said again. 'I mean, the Penroses were always so welcoming and Mrs. Penrose is a pillar of the church and leader of village society . . . '

'And all that' grinned Greg.

'And all that,' agreed Zoe, 'so how could she be involved in whatever's going on here?'

'All part of their carefully established, respectable cover,' said Greg. 'Successful crooks don't go about looking crooked, you know.'

'I'm still not convinced,' admitted Zoe. 'James has always been so kind. He came over the very first night I came because he saw a light and thought squatters might have moved into the cottage.'

'Well' said Greg, 'he wouldn't want squatters here anymore than he'd want you.'

'But what about when Aunt Jessie was here, he used to keep an eye on the place then, he even had . . . ' She paused in mid-sentence, put her hand to her mouth and then whispered, 'Oh, my God.'

'What?' said Gregory sharply. 'What's the matter?'

'He even had a key.'

'Come on,' said Greg immediately getting up from the table, 'let's put these in the kitchen and get to work.'

They carried the dirty dishes through to the kitchen and leaving them stacked on the draining board Greg picked up the hammer and chisel. Darkness had fallen and Zoe called Barney in from the garden before locking the back door.

'Pull the curtains and check the front door,' said Greg, 'and then we'll get going.'

Down in the cellar Gregory looked about him. 'Queen Anne's blocking the light a bit,' he said. 'We'll have to shift her further over.'

They edged the huge bookcase across the floor and Zoe said, 'I'm fed up with this great thing. I think I'll give it to your father.' Greg laughed and said, 'He'd love it, but don't do anything rash; it might be valuable.'

They turned their attention once more to the bricked up wall.

'There's no need to knock it all down to begin with, we'll just make a big enough hole to look through. I put a sledge-hammer in the car as well, but that's a bit drastic before we know if we need to break right through.'

Greg started chipping away at the mortar between the bricks. It came away quite easily and it was not long before he had several blocks loosened.

'Did he build it two bricks deep?'

'I don't know,' replied Zoe. 'I didn't come down while he was working.'

Greg went on chipping away until he was ready to move four bricks to leave a jagged hole in the wall.

'We'll need a torch to look through,' he said. 'It'll be dark the other side.'

Zoe went back upstairs to find the torch and as she reached the kitchen the phone began to ring. For a long moment she stood still listening to its insistent peel, but though she was tempted to answer to see if she could connect the muffled obscenities with James's cultured voice, she resisted. There was no point in letting the man know she was in, whoever it was; so leaving the bell shrilling alone she collected the flashlight and went back down to the cellar. As she reached the bottom of the steps the telephone stopped.

'I heard the phone,' said Greg, 'you didn't answer.'

'No, I knew it couldn't be you and there was no one else I wanted to talk to.' Gregory smiled at this but said nothing and turned back to his attack on the wall.

'Nearly big enough now, at least to get a head through.'

He had removed another brick and was working on another two. At length he slid them out and passed them back to the waiting Zoe who stacked them with the others. Then he took the torch and shone it through the aperture into the secret room. Zoe had replaced the exhausted batteries and it shone brightly, cutting through the darkness to show the room still furnished, but with half a bottle of milk and a loaf on the table, blankets on the camp bed and crouching in a corner, their dark eyes wide with fear, a woman and two children, one scarcely more than a baby.

Greg stared at them for a moment the beam of the torch never wavering from their faces. The older child put up a hand to shield his eyes from the light and the woman clutched the younger child to her, protecting its eyes against her.

'Hallo,' said Greg gently. 'Are you all right?'

The woman said nothing, pressing herself further into the corner, her children clinging to her.

Gregory turned to Zoe and told her what he had found.

Zoe peered in through the hole for a moment and then said, 'Come on Greg, we must get them out.'

18

Gregory fetched the sledgehammer from the car and it was not long before the hole in the wall was big enough for him to squeeze through. Zoe waited to help the woman and the children to creep out of their underground prison into the cellar. She took the smaller child in her arms while the mother eased her way through and Greg brought out the second child, a little Indian boy, shepherding him through.

'This baby's freezing,' said Zoe. 'We must get them upstairs and warm straight away.'

They clattered up the stairs and Zoe led them through into the sitting room where she immediately switched on the fire. So far the woman had said nothing. Now she managed a weary smile and 'Thank you'. She, too, was Indian. Her dark hair was wound round the back of her head and she was dressed in a sari with an overcoat on top. Zoe went into the kitchen to heat some soup and some milk while Greg put his jacket round the little boy and chafed his hands to bring some warmth to them. Gratefully all three gathered round the heat of the fire and when Zoe brought in the warm drinks they gulped them down. In the meantime Greg put Barney out in the garden to warn of anyone's approach.

Neither Greg nor Zoe asked any questions until they were sure their unexpected guests were getting warm, a little colour creeping back into their pinched faces. Zoe fetched a blanket for the little one and wrapped in it, full of warm milk, the child fell asleep in her mother's arms.

'Now,' said Greg at length, 'tell us what on earth you were doing in that terrible cellar.'

The woman looked at him seriously for a moment, as if deciding whether to trust him or not before she replied simply, 'I come to my husband.'

'Your husband?' repeated Zoe. 'Where is he?'

'He is living in Sheffield.'

'Sheffield! But that's hundreds of miles away.'

'But this is the only way. I bring my children to their father.'

'They're illegal immigrants,' said Greg. 'That's what James imports.'

The woman looked blank. 'We pay all our money. We have no more. You must take us to Sheffield. We have paid to go to Sheffield.'

'It's nothing to do with us,' said Gregory. 'We aren't involved in your journey. We shall have to pass you on to the police.'

'Not police,' cried the woman in alarm. 'You have our money. We must go to Sheffield.'

'We haven't got your money,' said Zoe gently. 'We don't know anything about you. All we did was find you in my cellar. This is my house.'

'How did you get here?' asked Greg.

'We came in a little ship from France and went to a big house. The children were afraid of the dark passages leading to our room.'

'How long have you been down there?' asked Zoe.

'I think we have three days there. It is hard to say, the light failed and we have seen nobody.'

'You mean no one has been back since you were left there?'

'An old woman came once and gave us more food, but after that the light went out and we have seen no one.'

'It's monstrous,' cried Zoe. 'Leaving you down there in the dark and cold!'

'They say they will come soon. They say they must wait for a van to come. They say it will take some days.'

'They must have arrived the evening I was at Shearwater House. Mrs. Penrose keeping me safely out of the way playing Scrabble as they came up the cliff path and were crossed over the cliff to the house.'

Greg nodded. 'Probably,' he agreed.

'And then when you were back here at the cottage, bring them inside the house, down to the cellar and out through the passages. You none the wiser though your cottage was still being used. But how much easier for them if you were not here at all; that's why they're determined to get you out.'

'How clever of you both to work it all out.' James's voice cut harshly through the room and they all spun round in horror to see him standing in the doorway with a small black automatic in his hand. 'Much too clever; in fact you've been nothing but a nuisance from the moment you arrived here, my dear Zoe. In other circumstances I could have grown quite fond of you, you have such a beautiful white body.' He laughed as he had laughed on the telephone and the last wisp of doubt that James Penrose had been the obscene caller left Zoe as she heard him and she shuddered as the lewdness even now crept into his voice. 'But' he continued, 'I will not have my business operations interfered with. What a pity you were so obstinate about moving.'

Zoe, surprisingly, was not scared at that moment, but extremely angry, maybe her anger drove out her fear, but she faced James and his gun squarely and said slowly and distinctly, 'You are a bastard, the lowest kind of mean bastard, trafficking in human beings.'

James remained unruffled and said smoothly, 'Anyone would think I was dealing in slaves. It's quite the opposite, I'm returning this lucky woman to the bosom of her husband. What could be more philanthropic? They have to put up with a little hardship it's true but what is that compared with the joy they'll have when they are reunited? And my commitment doesn't end there, I guarantee to protect them against any unwise person who might try to inform against them. A comprehensive service, you see.'

'Did you make use of the cottage in this dreadful manner when my aunt lived here?' asked Zoe angrily.

James gave a short laugh. 'Of course, that was simple. She was as deaf as a post, we could come and go as we chose once she was in bed. And you'd never have discovered anything if I'd been able to get in through the cellar and get Jarvis out. Who put that great bookcase across the door? That used to be this end of the cellar where the logs are now.'

Aware that Gregory was edging towards the light switch in the hope of plunging the room into darkness Zoe tried to keep James's attention on herself.

'So, she caught you out by having it moved so her logs could be nearer the steps. Well done, Aunt Jessie, even if it was unintentional. Now it's finally got you caught. You're found out, James Penrose, and you'll pay for it; you and your mother.'

'How very dramatic you are, my dear Zoe; pay for it indeed, truly quaint.' Without altering his condescending tone James remarked, 'If you move another inch, Enodoc, I'll put a bullet in your precious Zoe.'

Greg froze and Zoe went cold. She knew James would do as he said.

'Now it appears we have a problem,' went on James. 'I was taking these,' he indicated the woman and children cowering in the big armchair beside the fire, 'on the next leg of their journey. I don't really want to have to take you two as well. If you had stayed out all day as you had arranged you wouldn't have been in the way tonight, but as always you had to interfere. The only useful thing you've managed since you arrived was to discover the passage linking my house with yours. Now, I must consider what to do with you.' He never sounded more than mildly irritated, but there was something in his voice which made Zoe's blood run cold, something far more sinister than if he had raged at them. She knew he was ruthless and that she and Gregory stood in his way and she was desperately afraid for both of them.

Keeping his gun pointed straight at Zoe, James crossed to the telephone and, picking up the receiver, dialled. His eyes never still, flicked from Zoe to Greg and back again, giving neither a chance to make a move against him.

'Hallo, Mother. I've run into a little trouble here. I'm at the cottage. Zoe and Enodoc have found the merchandise. We shall have to alter our plans. I can't leave them so you'd better bring the van down here and put in a couple of extra laundry baskets.' He listened to his mother for a moment or two and then said testily, 'Don't worry, Mother, we'll discuss the details when you get here.' He replaced the receiver and with a jerk ripped the wire from the back of the phone. Then he turned and said to Zoe, 'We have a long journey, make a Thermos of coffee and some sandwiches. Thanks to you I shall not get to eat until tomorrow. By the way,' he added as Zoe moved slowly towards the kitchen, 'don't do anything stupid like trying to go for help, because if you make a break I shall shoot the baby.' The woman gave a little cry and clutched the still sleeping child even more closely to her.

'Don't worry,' said Zoe, looking at James with undisguised loathing, 'I shan't.'

She went into the kitchen and saw the cellar door standing open. She thought she had shut it behind her when they had brought the Indian family up into the cottage. Obviously James had approached the secret room from the underground passage side and finding the hole in the wall had quietly come on through it and up into the house. If only they had locked the cellar door, he could not have broken in on them without warning. Furious at their carelessness Zoe felt tears of rage pricking her eyes. She put on the kettle and while waiting for it to boil quickly made several rounds of cheese sand-wiches.

'What can we do? What can we do?' As always, under stress, she muttered to herself, her brain in a turmoil as she made and dismissed plans to save them all. Then, as she reached the coffee down from the shelf something caught her eye and gave her the glimmering of an idea. Quickly she filled the Thermos and put both the packet of sandwiches and the flask into a shopping basket. Then carefully, she took down another pot from the shelf and emptied its contents into the palm of her right hand and closed her fingers over it; then picking up the shopping basket in her left hand she returned to the living room.

James was explaining to the Indians that they would be travelling in a laundry van, packed into great wicker laundry baskets; he glanced at Zoe as she came in swinging the gun round to point at Gregory as she passed between himself and the threatened baby. Zoe calmly put the basket down on the chair beside James and as she straightened up with one swift action she flung a handful of pepper full in his face.

The gun went off with an echoing report as James clutched at his eyes. Greg fell to the floor with a sharp gasp, but Zoe, knowing she might have only a moment to act grabbed Ron the Rubber plant and using his stem as a handle, swung him into the air and crashed the pot on to James's head. The pot cracked, Ron's stem broke and James subsided quietly to the floor, the gun clattering down beside him. Zoe grabbed it and pointed it at James's head, but he did not move, she had knocked him unconscious. She turned to find Greg lying on the floor, his right hand clutching his left arm, where blood was seeping through his fingers and spreading in a brilliant stain across his shirt. His face was deathly pale and his eyes closed with pain. For a split second she thought he was dead and her heart contracted in agony, then he groaned and moved his head.

'Greg, darling!' she cried. 'You're hurt.' And she dropped to her knees beside him to cradle his head against her.

He opened his eyes and managed a faint grin. 'I'm all right. Where's Penrose?'

'Over there on the floor, he's unconscious.'

'Well done, sweetheart. Tie him up.'

'But your arm, what about your arm? You don't look all right at all.'

'I'll be fine for a minute or two, but you must get him tied up before he comes round. Got a washing line or something?'

Zoe got a piece of washing line from the kitchen and heaving James over none too gently on to his face, tied his hands behind his back and then without cutting the rope tied his feet as well so that he would be unable to move when he came round again. Gregory watched.

'Good girl,' he said. 'Now we must get ready for Mrs. Penrose.'

'Not till I've done something about your arm, you're bleeding all over the

310

place,' and despite his protests Zoe fetched a pile of clean tea towels from the kitchen and ripping away the blood soaked shirt sleeve carefully bound a pad made from one folded towel over the ugly gash with strips torn from two others. When she had finished she glanced down at Gregory's face, now a whiter shade of pale and without a word poured him a large measure of the medicinal brandy they had joked about earlier in the week. She held it to his lips and said firmly, 'Drink this, it'll do you good.' Obediently Greg gulped it down and a little colour began to creep back into his face.

Movement from the fireside made Zoe turn to the Indian family whom she had momentarily forgotten.

'You stay by the fire,' she said sharply. 'Don't move, you are not safe yet.'

'Depends which side they're on,' pointed out Greg. 'Don't forget they want to get to Sheffield, not to be handed over to the police.'

Zoe handed Greg the gun she had retrieved.

'You'd better cover them and James with that,' she advised. 'We don't want him coming round and shouting to warn his dear mother.'

'What are we going to do about her? We must get help.'

'I can't leave you alone here with them and the phone's no good. We'll have to deal with Mrs. Penrose when she arrives.'

'You will you mean,' said Greg ruefully. 'I'm not going to be much use to you, except to cover with James's gun.'

'You can't cover them all with that gun,' protested Zoe. 'We must immobilise Mrs. Penrose somehow. Wait a minute, I've got an idea.'

She rushed upstairs and returned with a blanket.

'When she arrives we'll hear the van, I'll unlatch the door and as she comes in I'll chuck the blanket over her head. I've brought the luggage strap from my big suitcase, I'll drop it over her head and pull it tight so that her arms are pinioned.'

'Doesn't sound very easy to me,' said Greg. 'Why not let her in and I'll cover her while you tie her up.'

'She may have a gun. If she's half expecting trouble I doubt if she'll walk in blindly. I don't think it'll be too difficult. I should have the element of surprise and she's smaller and older than I am.'

Greg was still dubious, but as he was unable to take any active part in the capture of Mrs. Penrose, he said, 'It's worth a try I suppose. I'll still have the gun in case of emergency. Better move Penrose out of her line of vision though,' he advised. 'Can you manage? God, I feel so helpless!'

'Of course I can,' said Zoe. 'Don't you move or you'll start losing more blood. Sit still.'

Greg grinned at her tone and said meekly, 'Yes, Mum.' Barney, still free in the garden suddenly began to bark.

'That must be Mrs. Penrose. Hurry, move James.'

Zoe grabbed James's feet and managed to drag him across the floor so that he was not immediately visible from the front door, then she picked up the blanket and the luggage strap, the end already through the buckle so she could pull it tight instantly. Quietly unlatching the front door she stood poised behind it. Barney continued to bark and then they heard a car engine, it stopped outside and a door slammed.

Mrs. Penrose made no sound as she approached the door but as the handle began to turn, the Indian woman who had continued to watch and listen from the armchair and knew Gregory and Zoe intended to give her up to the police, started to scream, long piercing screams that rose to a deafening crescendo as her children, terrified, joined in. Immediately, the door was flung wide and Mrs. Penrose moved in, incredibly fast for one of her age, a gun in her hand as with a glance she took in the situation, Greg wounded, James tied. But her sight was cut off as Zoe, from behind, threw the blanket over her head and as she floundered in its folds Zoe forced the looped strap down over Mrs. Penrose's shoulders and pulled it tight.

The gun she had been carrying clattered to the floor. The Indian woman was still screaming and Greg bellowed at her, 'Quiet! You stupid woman. Quiet.'

Nobody noticed Barney was still barking, nor that another car had drawn up outside. With a hard shove, Zoe pushed the struggling Mrs. Penrose into an armchair, where effectively blinded and constrained by the blanket and strap she remained, her feet paddling in her attempts to get up. Zoe then turned her attention to the still screaming Indian woman and with a sharp slap across her face silenced her hysteria, though the children were still in full cry. James, just coming round, groaned and then started to struggle as he discovered he was tied.

Through the general chaos a loud voice boomed and abruptly reduced the room to a stunned silence. Zoe spun round to see two sturdy uniformed policemen at the door and with all her strength suddenly draining from her she sank down on to the floor beside Gregory, who said, 'Thank God. It's the cavalry.'

'What on earth is going on here?' demanded one of the policemen. He looked at Greg with the gun in his hand, and said quietly, 'I'll take charge of that,' and did so. His colleague picked up the one Mrs. Penrose had dropped in her struggles with the blanket and then he said, 'Perhaps someone could explain exactly what has been going on.'

Zoe did so as briefly as she could, ending up by saying, 'Mr. Enodoc is hurt, he should go to hospital at once. The telephone's been cut off.'

'I'll radio for an ambulance,' said the

first policeman and went back to the panda car outside.

'What made you come here?' asked Zoe, still amazed by their timely arrival.

'We still have a tap on your phone, miss,' answered the policeman. 'Somebody made a call saying there was trouble here. It was not made to us of course, but we thought perhaps we should come and find out what was going on.'

'Thank God you did,' said Zoe with sincerity.

The police took the Penroses out to their car, P.C. Dewar arrived from the village in a second car and carried off the Indian family. The ambulance was on its way and when Greg was patched up and had had a good night's sleep the police would be back for a formal account of the whole affair.

Zoe closed the front door behind P.C. Dewar, locked the fateful cellar door and went back into the living room where Greg, still very pale had been made as comfortable as possible in the armchair by the fire. He smiled as she came in and indicated Ron lying on the floor, his stem snapped and his pot cracked and leaking soil.

'You haven't done him much good.'

Zoe shrugged and said with a laugh, 'Robert gave him to me, I knew he'd come in useful some day. I'll chuck him out tomorrow.'

'I'll buy you another if you like,' offered Greg. Zoe shook her head and with a wry grin admitted, 'I don't really like house plants. I only brought him to spite Rosemary.'

She went across to Greg's chair and pulled up the tuffet to sit beside him. She looked at his face so pale yet so strong and said a little awkwardly, 'Greg, what does a girl say when she's been an idiot and made a mistake about how she feels?' Greg captured her hands in his sound hand and held them gently, his eyes intent on her face. 'Are you saying what I hope you're saying, sweetheart?'

Zoe nodded.

'In that case,' said Greg, 'you say 'Greg I . . . ' ' He stopped and said gruffly, 'Hell, Zoe, how do I know what you say? I only know what I want to say. Sweetheart, I love you, every brave and beautiful inch of you. I've loved you since you first walked into my life and without you there'd be no more life.'

Zoe felt her heart leap at his words; she had seen him lying on the floor his eyes closed and blood on his clothes and for one brief moment she had thought him dead. That moment was enough to shatter all her defences as she realised how she would feel if that had indeed been so. Now she knew with an absolute certainty that she loved and wanted Greg passionately and that life would be nothing to her without him. That he should feel, and actually say, the same thing to her was altogether so wonderful that she could find no words to answer him. She raised her eyes to his, so brilliant, still watching her intently and very gently so as not to jolt his injured arm, reached up and kissed him. Injured or not, his response was immediate. His good arm reached round her and held her firmly to him as he returned her kiss with a passion that matched her own and left her in no doubt of the depth of his feeling. When he released her at last he said softly, 'Oh, sweetheart!' and she saw her happiness mirrored in his eyes and her joy was complete; and so, each totally immersed in the other and their future together, they sat and waited for the ambulance.

We do hope that you have enjoyed reading this large print book.

Did you know that all of our titles are available for purchase?

We publish a wide range of high quality large print books including:
Romances, Mysteries, Classics
General Fiction
Non Fiction and Westerns

Special interest titles available in large print are:
The Little Oxford Dictionary
Music Book, Song Book
Hymn Book, Service Book

Also available from us courtesy of Oxford University Press:
Young Readers' Dictionary
(large print edition)
Young Readers' Thesaurus
(large print edition)

For further information or a free brochure, please contact us at:
Ulverscroft Large Print Books Ltd.,
The Green, Bradgate Road, Anstey,
Leicester, LE7 7FU, England.
Tel: (00 44) **0116 236 4325**
Fax: (00 44) **0116 234 0205**

Other titles in the
Linford Romance Library:

THE SLOPES OF LOVE

Diney Delancey

Recovering from a broken engagement, Karen Miller takes a job as resort representative at St. Wilhelm in Austria. Working at the Hotel Adler, she finds herself constantly at odds with the owner, the cold and distant Karl Braun. The guests arrive for the Christmas and New Year holidays, but behind the jollity of the festivities lurks danger — a sinister threat reaching out from England — which Karen must face alone in the cold darkness of the mountain.